THE
MONEY
HUNTERS

Other Books by Cothburn O'Neal

Pa

The Gods of Our Time

Hagar

Untold Glory

The Very Young Mrs. Poe

The Dark Lady

Master of the World

THE
MONEY
HUNTERS

a novel by

Cothburn O'Neal

CROWN PUBLISHERS, INC.   NEW YORK

THE
MONEY
HUNTERS

1

$ $ $

"SHE'D BE GOOD FOR FIFTY OR A HUNDRED THOUSAND, IF WE could get to her, but she won't even talk to us," Brother Hilliard, the campaign chairman, said despondently. "And her family practically built our present church. Gave the money, that is."

"Why won't she see you?" Larry asked, as he sat at his desk in a corner of Campaign Headquarters in the fellowship hall of Calvary Church and listened to Brother Hilliard's Saturday-morning comments on the well-heeled citizens of Batesville who had so far evaded the fund raiser's bite.

"It goes way back, to that sissy son of hers who used to sing tenor in the choir. He was a mama's boy clear through. It was a long time before he started noticing other girls. But he finally did; only he didn't get married. One night the sexton found him with the organist right here in the sanctuary, after they had stayed late to rehearse his solo for Sunday morning."

Larry cluck-clucked at the shame of it. "Seems I've heard that story before, but as I remember, it was usually the choir-master and the organist."

"Anyway, old Jarvis came around to lock up; and when he heard noises in the dark church he turned on the lights.

Well, there they were, about where the coffin usually rests during a funeral."

"So that was their funeral."

"Not for a few days. But old Jarvis herded them into the pastor's study and telephoned their parents and the preacher. It was all over Batesville by morning. Weldon—that was his name—hung himself the next Sunday morning, and Old Lady Bates hasn't been in this church since."

"Tragic," Larry said.

"Yeah. Like I said, she'd be good for fifty or a hundred thousand dollars—all of it, in fact, if we could only get to her."

"Shall I try to see her?" The ace field director for Christian Benevolences, Inc., had softened up harder ones in his time.

"I say you won't get anywhere."

"Why not?"

"Well, you can try, but she seldom sees anybody, especially not from this church. She reads the newspaper, though, and she'll know you're directing our fund drive, and what you want."

"I'll think about it." Larry was already thinking that he smelled the Anonymous Donor in Old Lady Bates. He had three other prospects for that bit of money hunter's magic, but they were pikers compared to Agatha Bates.

"Do that," the Campaign Manager said, rising, "and let me know how you come out—as if I didn't know already."

Larry kept calculating eyes on Brother Hilliard's back until they were pleasantly diverted by the sight of Pat Hayden, who entered the fellowship hall as the Campaign Manager was leaving. She headed for Larry's desk, but paused to admire the architect's perspective of the new Calvary Church—the focal point of Campaign Headquarters.

Pat Hayden was young, healthy, and efficient. He liked her the first time he saw her, when she came into Campaign Headquarters that Monday morning—fresh, enthusiastic, aglow at the prospect of a fine new Calvary Church with a whole wing designed especially for youth activities.

"I'm Patricia Hayden—Pat to friends," she said by way of greeting, the breeze through open windows shaping her light summer dress to fit her figure, lithe, trim, and firm.

"Laurence Shelton—"

"Oh, yes, Mr. Shelton, I know."

"Larry to friends." He grasped her outstretched hand.

"Isn't it going to be wonderful?" She indicated the architect's drawing.

"Beautiful," Larry agreed.

"And functional," she added practically. "By the way, I'm the youth director, but Dr. Briggs says that I'm to be your leg man during the campaign." Completely unself-conscious, but most admirably equipped for leg work.

"You should be a centipede," Larry said. "Everybody is a legman in a fund drive."

She laughed at that, but her eyes were still on the picture of the church. That left room for his eyes on her, and there they roamed: over her crisp bronze curls cropped almost as close as his—in the days of the beehive, too—over her clean scrubbed profile, her tanned neck and arms, and the high rise of her bosom.

"You're sure we can raise *all* the money for it," she said, flashing her clear blue eyes, momentarily worried, at his face for an instant.

"Positive," he said.

"I do hope so. It's been our dream—mine and the kids'—for so long. And you know how dreams are. They so seldom come true."

"This one will," he had assured her.

He could still give her that assurance, but little girls had to be taught to wait anxiously for their goodies; and he had to remember his code. Never let it look too easy.

Pat finished her brief adoration of the masterpiece and proceeded to Larry's desk.

3

"Pfc. Hayden reporting for duty, sir." She saluted smartly and remained at attention in a light summer dress, which, though green, bore not the slightest resemblance to G.I. fatigues.

"O.K., First Class. I presume you have the command car outside."

"Gassed, oiled, greased, and watered. Where do we go today?"

"Do you think Betsy can climb the hill this morning?"

"You mean to the old Bates mansion?" Pat's banter was gone.

"The very same."

"Yes. She can make it. Do you have to? I mean, are they wishing *her* off on you?"

"Seems I've been elected." He rose and came around the desk to join her.

"Do we have to call on her? Is—is the drive so hopeless that we have to ask her for money?"

"That's not quite the situation."

"But Old Mrs. Bates—her case is such a sad one."

They had reached the door.

"Then you know the story," Larry said on the way to Pat's car.

"Of course. One can't live long in Batesville without hearing it. And a thing like that leaves such a scar on a congregation, and on the church itself. It's unfair, but people still point out the building where they—" Pat blushed—the only time Larry had ever seen her embarrassed. "Can't we just leave her be?"

"I'd like to talk to her, if I can. Obviously she's a sentimentalist. She might want to give something in memory of her son."

"To replace the sanctuary he profaned? Oh, Larry, the congregation would never allow a memorial—a window or a tablet or anything—not for him. They're still so conscious of the scandal, after all these years."

4

Pat drove up the hill to the gate of an iron fence encircling the spacious unkempt grounds of the Bates mansion.

"I'll just get out here," Larry said.

"Shall I wait for you?"

"No. I can walk back. It's downhill all the way."

"I think I wish you luck, Larry. But it's so sad, so tragic. Anyway, I don't envy you." She smiled wanly as he closed the car door.

He tried the gate. It was not locked, but it was rusty from disuse and hard to open. He made his way through a full summer's growth of dead weeds, a hundred yards or more, to the front door of the Victorian monstrosity. He twisted the handle of an archaic doorbell and heard the unmusical clang on the inside.

For a moment he heard nothing more. Then a sound like that of a penny whistle came somewhere from his left. He located the funnel of an old-fashioned speaking tube in the doorjamb. It had been placed for shorter people than he, but he stooped, pressed the little bell crank sticking out of the side of the funnel, and blew into the pipe with all the breath he could muster. It left him somewhat dizzy.

"Who is it?" a dry, cracked voice asked when he placed his ear to the funnel.

"A friend of Weldon's."

"You can't be. He passed on years ago."

"I might be. I'm a stranger to you and Batesville, but I might be a friend of Weldon's."

"What do you want?"

"I want to talk to you—about Weldon."

There was a long pause. Then the old voice crackled again.

"I'll be down in a minute."

It was much longer than a minute, but eventually the door opened a crack, and Larry felt eyes looking him up and down and over. Slowly the door opened wider.

"Come in, young man," Agatha Bates said. "You're lying

5

to me. You're much too young to have known Weldon, but come on in." Her voice was younger than it had sounded through the speaking tube.

"I didn't say I knew him. I said I was a friend of his. I may be."

Larry entered the dark, musty hallway. He would have bet that there was a parlor with a harmonium, a stereoscope, and a vase of decomposed rose leaves. But he never got to the parlor. Agatha Bates seated him on a bare, uncushioned settee in the hall and sat down beside him.

"Well, what is it?" she asked.

As his eyes adjusted to the dim light, Larry found Old Mrs. Bates not without grace or charm, and far from a crackpot.

"I have been employed by Calvary Church to raise funds for a sanctuary and education building," he said frankly.

"Did they send you to see me?"

"No. The Campaign Manager advised against it."

She nodded. "I haven't been inside that church in twenty years."

"I know."

"Everybody knows. They think I'm crazy. They think I'm going to hell."

"Are you?" Larry risked the impudence.

"What a question!" Her eyes were alert and intelligent, but strange, now that Larry could see them. "No. I've been there. What's your name?"

"Laurence Shelton. Laurence P. Shelton."

"For Peter?"

"Yes."

"My son's middle name was Peter. Peter was a weak man, but a good man. So was Weldon."

"I share their weakness."

"Are you a good man, Mr. Shelton?"

"No."

"I think perhaps you are. And I don't think you're lying

to me. You might have been a friend of Weldon's if he had lived. You wanted to talk about him. Tell me."

"I wanted to solicit a gift to the building fund of Calvary Church. Don't you want to give something in memory of your son?"

"Oh, I couldn't. At the time I was so ashamed that I shut myself away. Not of Weldon. He was weak. Ashamed of me. I spoiled him. I sheltered him. I protected him. I made him weak and dependent. If I gave money to the church now, they would say I was trying to buy his way out of purgatory, and —well, we in Calvary Church don't believe in purgatory." Pretty reasonable for a demented recluse.

"No one need ever know. You have kept Weldon alive all these years in your heart. You can build his memory into the new church without anyone but you ever knowing about it."

"Now, Mr. Shelton. They know you have come here. If you suddenly produced a sizable donation they would know where it came from. Batesville is a small place. Everybody would know. I couldn't stand that. I've overcome my shame, but I still have my pride. I can't seem to overcome it. I couldn't help the church and have them talking again."

"I can arrange anonymity."

"How? Tell me how, and don't lie to me."

"I won't lie to you, and I won't have to lie to them. My boss should be in town in a few days. He can arrange for you to make your gift through his office so that no one but the tax people will ever know. He does it all the time. Then I can truthfully say that I never got a penny from you."

"Yes, you could say that."

"In fact, I can leave without your even promising anything. Not even I need ever know what transpires between you and David Chancellor."

"There are devious ways of keeping oneself honest, aren't there, Mr. Shelton?" She smiled, and the strangeness seemed to have gone from her eyes.

7

"Indeed there are." Larry left after that. He was sure that David Chancellor had the AD in his pocket.

The victory rankled in Larry's mind all the way downhill into town. He, single-handed, did the pick-and-shovel work, and then set up the pins for David Chancellor's strike on the day of his Appearance. He, Laurence P. Shelton, could have closed out the Calvary Church campaign with a surplus by the middle of the past week and could have been back in New York already. With his list of prospects and his know-how he could still go over the top in any given twelve hours of daylight, without benefit of Old Lady Bates. But, oh, no, it would appear too easy to the volunteer workers; it would violate the code of the National Association of Fund Raisers; worst of all, it would obviate the necessity for Kind David's Appearance and the heaven-sent Anonymous Donor.

Larry tortured himself with the vision of David Chancellor.

There he sat at his desk in the Home Office, beyond the Round Table, where Christian benevolences were discussed in all piety and cupidity. Good old-fashioned David Chancellor, his handsome face glowing with divinity beneath the thick white mane haloed by the morning sun shining through the Church Street windows, his hands placed precisely, finger tips to finger tips, in front of his black vest with the anachronistic white piping down its V—a bishop in anybody's diocese, a son of a bishop, a vain moneygrubber, jealous of his image, jealous of his successful field directors, jealous of his position as founder and dean of NAFR, jealous of life at sixty-nine.

The vision of the Master drew Larry's mind back to his own plight, another week end in Batesville. Nary a drink, nary a dame. The very thought began to sap his confidence in the future. *Non sequitur* of course, but he had a rule of thumb that every million dollars raised should carry a bonus of at least one eager bedmate sufficiently infatuated with his genius. Dolls and dollars had a natural affinity, especially in the stories

8

told around the NAFR campfires when that particular breed of liars congregated for the good of the order.

Before succumbing entirely to self-pity, he reminded himself that as the Calvary Church drive was only a half-million-dollar campaign, he was entitled to only half a woman at best. But the three available ones he had spotted among the campaign workers exceeded half a woman each by at least a hundred per cent. And the fourth—not tabbed as available even in his most optimistic estimates—could well be quoted at several times the going rate: Patricia Hayden, Miss Health of Any Year.

And Pat was the first person he saw when he re-entered the fellowship hall. She let him get settled at his desk before she sauntered over and asked, almost conspiratorially, "How did you come out?"

"Not a penny."

"In a way I'm glad, though I hope we don't wind up short."

"We won't."

Pat wandered away. She had been very careful not to show Larry too much attention. Now he knew why: Calvary Church could not stand another scandal, and Batesville was a small town and people would talk for twenty years.

It being Saturday, Larry spent the afternoon going over the confidential figures on Calvary Church campaign. The estimates had to be exact. There was little margin for error: money on hand, gifts pledged, pushovers remaining, positive data on the Anonymous Donor.

They had to balance. That is, the apparent deficit had to approximate the amount known to be forthcoming from the Anonymous Donor. And they seemed to be in balance. The deficit, after the remaining pushovers had been pushed, showed up as being around fifty thousand dollars; and Old Lady Bates was good for that much.

Next he proofread Pat's typed copy of the Third Week's Progress Report, which he had prepared for the Campaign

9

Chairman—a masterly document beginning with unbounded praise and enthusiasm for the work already accomplished, shading into hope for continued success, and finally injecting just enough doubt to spur the workers to more strenuous effort and to arouse incipient uneasiness in the more niggardly consciences among Dr. Briggs's flock.

When Campaign Headquarters closed, Pat drove him to the Bates Hotel. After a dull dinner he went to a movie and then to bed, abstinent and alone.

2

$ $ $

AT THE MORNING SERVICE LARRY SAT BESIDE BROTHER HILLIARD, who, in anticipation of reading the Third Week's Progress Report, fidgeted restlessly throughout Dr. Briggs's sermon on the text, "It is more blessed to give." He took the negative report on Old Lady Bates as the fulfillment of his personal prophecy, and but for his long discipline in the silence of the sanctuary, he would probably have sought whispered reassurances from Larry every few minutes. Larry did nothing to allay the good brother's nervousness, however. It was part of the act.

Dr. Briggs ended his homily with the announcement of a brief business meeting to be held before the closing hymn. He called on Brother Hilliard for his report. The Campaign

Chairman began self-consciously, but seemed heartened by the first part of Larry's paper. He gradually warmed to his task and earnestly exhorted his co-workers to redoubled effort during the final week of the drive; but then he succumbed to the uneasiness Larry had written into the last few paragraphs. The congregation stayed right with him, reflecting his every mood—especially his growing concern as his voice trailed off dispiritedly in the concluding sentences.

The effect—as planned—was such that Dr. Briggs called a brief meeting of the Church Board and the Key Personnel in his study immediately after the service. Even the closing hymn sounded more dirgelike than had been originally intended.

"How do you feel about the progress of the campaign, Larry?" Dr. Briggs asked when the group had crowded into his study.

"Well, we're over a hundred thousand dollars behind," Larry admitted, forcing a despondency he did not feel.

"Not much over a hundred thousand," Pat Hayden said with a degree of optimism not apparent in her face.

"But over a hundred thousand," Larry went on, "and most of the cream has already been skimmed off. The last hundred thousand is admittedly the hardest, the last week the slowest. It's true in all campaigns."

"Do you have any suggestions?" Brother Hilliard allowed his question to sound like a challenge.

"Yes—yes, I have one," Larry said reluctantly.

"What is it?" Dr. Briggs said.

"Frankly, Dr. Briggs, I think we should call in Mr. Chancellor to tackle some of these good people who are wavering."

"Mr. Chancellor himself?" Dr. Briggs had sat at the Round Table in the Home Office. "Would he come down, really?"

"Yes, Dr. Briggs, I think he would. If I know David Chancellor, and I believe I do, he'll drop whatever he's doing and

11

catch the first plane down here, once he knows that Calvary Church is experiencing some difficulty in this campaign."

"Mr. Chancellor made no such agreement when we talked to him." Brother Hilliard still doubted. "It's not in our contract."

"But I'm almost sure he'll do it," Larry said. "And, of course, he never makes any extra charge for his personal services."

The sighs of relief were clearly audible.

"If you think he would—" Dr. Briggs began.

"Let me try him. I'll tell you what I'll do. I'll go right to my hotel and call him at home—he should be back from church by the time I get there. If any man can pull us out of this hole, it's David Chancellor."

Larry did not unduly emphasize *man*, but he got the desired response.

"I think, too," the Campaign Chairman said uneasily, "that we should call together our corps of workers for a session of prayer after the evening service. Dr. Briggs?"

"By all means. I'll have my secretary do a little phoning this afternoon. And Larry, you will call Mr. Chancellor?"

"Indeed I will."

The meeting broke up, and the Key Personnel departed with varying degrees of hope in their hearts.

"I have my car," Pat said to Larry. "I'll drive you back to your hotel."

"Thanks," Larry said, and fell into step beside her on the way to the parking lot.

"Are you really worried, Larry?" she asked as he opened her car door for her.

"I think it's time Mr. Chancellor was called in," he said. Why was he not allowed to do the grandstanding sometimes? At least this once, with Miss Health and Recreation in the gallery.

"What do you mean, 'time Mr. Chancellor was called in'?" she asked when he was seated beside her.

12

"It's some of the Big Gifts, Pat, the fifteen or twenty big givers who account for seventy or eighty per cent of the total—my responsibility. The workers are doing fine. I'm the one who needs help."

"But that's absurd! I know that you've raised about three hundred thousand dollars already," Pat insisted staunchly. "That is, you've *helped* some picked workers bring that much in on silver platters. They've been given the credit; but don't think for a minute that I don't know who engineered the approaches."

"You learn too fast," he said, laughing, but conscious of the bitterness in his own remark. He and Pat could take her little blue sedan and raise another hundred and fifty thousand before bedtime, if she only knew.

"We're short, and time is getting shorter," he said with finality.

"But I'm sure you could raise the money, *all* of it. I've banked on you so heavily—and—well, I've never met Mr. Chancellor—I've never seen him in action. And we must have *all* of it."

"He'll get all of it." And keep fifteen per cent, Larry added to himself.

"Here we are," Pat said, pulling up to the yellow curb at the hotel entrance.

"How about having lunch with me?"

"I don't know if I should," she said cautiously.

"You're twenty-one."

"Twenty-two."

"All right, twenty-two, and respectable. We'll get a table by a window so that everyone in Batesville can see there's nothing sneaky going on."

"O.K. I'll call Mrs. Durham and tell her not to wait dinner on me."

"You do that while I call New York."

They left the car to the doorman and entered the lobby together. Pat went into a booth, and Larry used a house telephone to get his New York number through the hotel switchboard.

David Chancellor answered after two rings.

"Larry Shelton," Larry said.

"Glad to hear from you, my boy. I knew who it was when I heard Batesville on the line."

"All systems *go*."

"Don't be flippant, Larry."

"O.K.," Larry said, and then went on with mock formality. "The Campaign Chairman of Calvary Church feels that the fund drive is not progressing as well as it might. The board has urged me to invite you down to lend us a hand."

"I shall be delighted to help. I'll be down by the first plane in the morning. Let me see—it arrives there about ten thirty, I believe." He ought to know. He already had his ticket in his pocket, or he was losing confidence in his ace field director.

"We'll meet you then, sir," Larry said. "At ten thirty."

Pat, having completed her call, was approaching Larry as he put the receiver down.

"Did you get Mr. Chancellor?" she asked.

"Oh, yes. He'll be here on the ten-thirty flight tomorrow morning. Does Mrs. Durham approve of your scandalous escapade?"

"Don't make fun of me, Larry. I have to be careful here." She looked straight ahead as she preceded him into the dining room. "I've always had to be careful. As a youth director in Christian service—well, I just can't allow any room for gossip. I have to be above suspicion or I'm no good at all. We can't risk another scandal in this church."

"Sorry, Pat. I wasn't making fun of you. Teasing, yes— but I meant no offense." And to his surprise, Larry believed himself. He felt ever so protective toward this model for a *Playboy* pin-up devoted to Christian service.

Obviously there was one thing Pat did not have to be careful about—her diet. Larry could not remember when he had

14

lunched with a woman who showed less concern for calories. She ordered the special chicken dinner with all the trimmings and methodically began working her way through it.

"What is Mr. Chancellor like?" she asked.

"He is a fine pious gentleman of the old school"—Larry might as well let her have the Image—"as devoted to his field of Christian service as you are to yours. He loves his work, loves pruning the Master's vineyard," and reaping the harvest thereof, he added mentally while continuing aloud. "You'll see. He inspires hope and confidence even in those of little faith. Once he makes his appearance in Batesville, our troubles will dissipate like mist before the morning sun." A little strong perhaps, but it should enhance the Image.

Pat frowned slightly, at least subconsciously aware of something wrong in Larry's description.

"But does he share your enthusiasm?" she asked. "The enthusiasm you have shown until—until this morning."

"Share my enthusiasm? He sparks my enthusiasm. He's the heart and soul of Christian Benevolences, has been for forty years. He pioneered guided philanthropy in this country and has long been in the forefront, directing Christian giving everywhere."

"Don't you want him to come here?" Pat was not all dumb.

"I suggested his coming. I called him and asked him to come."

"You didn't answer my question. Do you want him to come? Will he really be of any help? You're different today, you know, as if you have given up."

"Of course I want him to come. Yes, he will really help us out. He'll fire the campaign workers with a zeal such as you've never dreamed of."

"Will he fire you if the drive falls short of its goal?" Pat was direct.

Larry had to laugh at that. Then he began soberly: "Look, Pat. There isn't the remotest possibility of our falling short of our goal. No matter how dark things look today, or to-morrow, or Wednesday, or even next Saturday, we'll go over the top, with money to spare. Take my word for it."

"I will," Pat said, just as soberly. "That's what I want—your word for it, Larry. I trust you. I have confidence in you. I've seen you in action, and I know what you can do. I just don't want you to let down when Mr. Chancellor comes—as you seem to have done already. We can't fail; we just *can't*. That's why I risked having lunch with you, to reassure myself. I'd do almost anything, risk anything to get our church, with those wonderful facilities for youth work."

"So it wasn't my charm, after all."

"It was that, too," Pat answered his smile. "You have charm, all right, and strength and genius—and you have them under control. Just don't let me down, Larry. Don't. No, not *me*. *Us*. Don't let the kids down."

Wait till you meet David Chancellor, young lady, Larry all but mumbled. If only he, Laurence P. Shelton, could be allowed the big play, he would show her and the kids.

Pat polished off her big slice of pie topped with whipped cream, and showed no hesitation in accepting a second glass of milk. But not a calory showed in the wrong place when Larry held her chair and then followed her out into the lobby. If she ate that way every day—and she probably did—she was living proof of a Divine Plan for caloric intake and distribution.

3

$ $ $

A DOZEN OR MORE OF THE FAITHFUL—IN THREE CARS—WERE ON
hand for The Appearance when flight 63 touched down at ten
twenty-seven the next morning. It was a bright, late-August
morning promising heat, but with a breeze, before the day
was over. The airport was practically deserted except for the
small band of pilgrims, and David Chancellor was the only
deplaning passenger.

He would not have had it otherwise. Indeed, the yellow
sunshine turned the roll-away ramp into golden stairs as the
great man descended, his white silk suit and fine shock of
white hair equally dazzling in the light reflected by the alumi-
num fuselage. Halfway down to earth he recognized Dr.
Briggs and his committee; then a beatific smile lighted up his
handsome face, and he raised his right hand in a blessing on
those below.

"Dr. Briggs, Brother Hilliard," he greeted in his rich
ecclesiastical baritone as he paused on the last step to shake
hands. He called the name of every man he had met before,
and acknowledged introductions to the others. Suddenly all
was right in the world, including Batesville.

"I don't believe I've met you, young lady," he said, ap-

17

proaching Larry and Pat, who had waited outside the circle of Powers and Dominions.

"I'm Pat Hayden," she said when he took her hand. "Larry's chauffeur and legman."

"Lucky Larry," he said, allowing his eyes to devour Pat in one comprehensive ogle before turning them on Larry.

"Good to see you, my boy." He extended a hand. "It will be fine working with you again for a day or two."

"We're glad to have you, sir." Larry said. "We're in need of the Master's touch, I'm afraid."

"I like to keep a hand in, for old times' sake. How I envy you the joy you must have found in your day-by-day association with these good people as they build God's kingdom." His speech was for the committee, his eyes furtively for Pat, his envy for Larry quite real.

"We're having lunch together," Dr. Briggs announced. "The Women's Service Group has prepared a repast for us in the deacon's room. Then the committee will be at your service—and you'll probably want some time with Larry."

"Yes, yes. I'm sure your fears are unfounded, but we'll have our chat and see what modifications, if any, are indicated in the campaign."

David Chancellor surrendered his baggage check to Larry and Pat and allowed himself to be herded toward Dr. Briggs's automobile.

"Somehow, I do feel better already," Pat said on the way to the luggage counter.

"I thought you would." Larry could feel a twinge of jealousy himself. And he could imagine what it might be like at sixty-nine.

"Oh, don't misunderstand me," Pat continued hastily. "I think you could have done all right by yourself; but I can see what comfort you might find in having Mr. Chancellor here to back you up."

"Yes, indeed. He's quite a comfort. Now if you'll just

drop me off at the hotel," Larry said as they went out to Pat's car.

"Aren't you going to the luncheon?"

"No. The committee must be given a chance to tell David Chancellor what's wrong with me."

"Oh no! They wouldn't."

"Oh yes, they will." He grinned.

"I mean, there's nothing wrong with the way you're handling the campaign."

"You're a loyal little coot, aren't you?"

"No. I mean yes. I mean I was given the job of helping you. And that's what I'm doing. That's the way I am, I guess."

"That's the way you are."

Larry took David Chancellor's bag inside the hotel and went up to his own room. He could not resist reviewing his conversation with Old Lady Bates. He recounted it word by word. Agatha Bates was primed for David Chancellor, who would get her money in half an hour. Larry would have liked to hear the dean of NAFR make his pitch. It would be a good one, he was sure, but he would never know.

The fat-cat money hunters never revealed all their tricks to the field directors, who were taught just enough to make them worth their hire, not enough to make them real threats to the top echelon. He wondered if the big boys swapped stories around their campfires the way the field hands did, bragging a bit, laughing at the gullibility of the gracious givers. More than likely they never showed a crack in their pious façades even to one another.

Larry ate lunch in the hotel coffee shop and walked back to Campaign Headquarters, which at the moment was unusually quiet—in a temporary lull, but tense with expectation pending the exodus from the deacon's room. The three available ones were there, and each in her own way communicated her presence to Larry. He moved about from table to table, keeping his own voice low and doing nothing to break the spell.

The committee passed through Campaign Headquarters on its way to the pastor's study. David Chancellor allowed himself to be introduced to the skeleton staff on duty, charming each one as he acknowledged the introduction. Larry watched his every move, and noted his expression as he shook hands with the available ones, and by God he spotted each of them instantaneously. The old boy had not lost his touch. He must have been a whale of a field hand in his day. He certainly had the money hunter's unerring sixth sense that told him at a glance what any man, woman, or child would deliver on demand.

After the Master had passed, Larry busied himself with a pack of pledge cards to shut out the buzz of *oh*'s and *ah*'s the Great One left in his wake. He was glad Pat had not been there to witness the Second Coming; but of course this was absurd. It was simply that the old goat got his goat. But when the gifts were totaled, Christian Benevolences, Inc., would get fifteen per cent of the gross, and Laurence P. Shelton would get ten per cent of that, which would not be bad for a month's work—even in Batesville. He could afford to play second fiddle to David Chancellor for two or three days a month.

Volunteer workers began returning from their lunch-hour interviews, and the hum of Campaign Headquarters grew busier and steadier as David Chancellor had his little chat with Dr. Briggs and the committee. By the time the confidential session was over, a little before three o'clock, all the work force was present, expectantly awaiting the next divine fiat. An awesome silence stopped the hum when the door to the pastor's study opened and the Shining One walked among them once again.

Dr. Briggs called his flock to prayer, but allowed David Chancellor to say the words. And he did, in tones so powerful and sonorous that a God who would not listen to them must have been deaf indeed. The campaign workers heard themselves blessed and commended for their labors. They felt the spirit enter their bodies and sensed the moment when they received the guidance invoked on their behalf. The benediction brought personal epiphany to every mortal intelligence in the crowded room. Larry had to admit that the old man got you—*there*—if you did not watch him. *Magister dixit.*

Pat turned moist eyes to Larry and smiled up at him after the resonant *Amen.* She had been had emotionally.

David Chancellor spoke briefly. He had already cast his spell. He needed only to make suggestions while the workers were under hypnosis. His voice was soft, lower than the tones employed in addressing the great beyond, but it still filled the room with confidence and enthusiasm.

"Now," he said in closing, "I must talk awhile with Larry and spend a few hours in meditation. In the morning we shall all be gleaners together and bring in the last scattered grains of our bountiful harvest."

The natural thing was for Pat to drive the two money hunters to their hotel. Larry was relegated to the back seat of the little blue sedan, where he was privileged to watch Mr. Benevolence charm Miss Health into harmony with the Sublime.

After settling himself briefly in his own quarters, David Chancellor came to Larry's room, where the master file was. Two human beings would have ordered drinks, but the minions of Mammon sat down to their conference dry.

"How does it look?" Larry asked his boss.

"In good order, as usual. How do you feel about it?"

"No sweat. We could have closed out last week if I had had the word."

"Now, now, my boy, you misunderstand the reasons for not moving too fast. Building a new church is a labor of love. The actual fund drive itself is a rich and rewarding experience for the workers involved, a task to be savored, to be prolonged, lingered over. It is a joy which will come to most of these people only once in a lifetime. Let us not rush them through a period of dedicated service, but give them time to secure

21

a sacred memory which they will cherish through all the days of their lives."

Unconsciously, David Chancellor had placed his hands, finger tips to finger tips, across his trim belly—or if he had done it consciously he was wasting his pious mannerism on his present audience.

"Yes, sir," Larry agreed.

"Now, about these recalcitrant givers," Chancellor began.

"The six pushovers I sent briefs on are good for ten to fifteen thousand apiece. You can solicit any one of them in thirty or forty minutes, I believe—handle them all in a day."

"Tut, tut, Larry. I detect a cynicism in your remarks that is highly unbecoming a member of the Christian Benevolences staff. I trust that this is not your usual manner of speech."

"You may trust that it is not, sir."

"Then I suggest that you cultivate the proper manner even in your most intimate conversations, if only to lessen the possibility of a verbal slip sometime."

"I understand perfectly."

"Good. I will say that I have never detected this fault in you before—around the home office, or in the field. A usually healthy flippancy, yes, but nothing offensive up until now. Are you really despondent? Worried about the campaign? Mrs. Bates, perhaps?"

"No, sir. Not at all." To be worried about Old Lady Bates would be to show lack of confidence in the head man. "I have told you about Mrs. Bates. She's primed. You'll have to stop her, not push her."

"Capital, capital. As it should be." David Chancellor nodded his approval. Even in rebuke he could be gracious and benign, quick to forgive a fault and commend a virtue. "I have already been in communication with Mrs. Bates, by telephone. She will see me at seven this evening, a social call. She is quite sensitive in the area of guided philanthropy, as you know, and she would not wish my visit to become common knowledge. I shall, of course, respect her wishes. I shall drop by her house on my customary evening stroll this very night."

"Certainly, sir." Larry had to admire the old bastard.

"Do you have any further suggestions on the other prospects?"

"No, sir. It's all in their dossiers. I'm sure that nothing I could add would be of any help to you."

"One more favor, Larry. I wonder if I could borrow your chauffeur for the next day or two. I find her a most charming young lady, undoubtedly quite familiar with the city and perhaps acquainted with the people I am to call upon." David Chancellor's eyes held the hint of a challenge as he made his request.

"Why, certainly. Of course. She's a free agent, and everything you have presumed her to be."

"Thank you, my boy. Now I think I'll lie down for an hour before dressing for my appointment with Mrs. Bates." He rose, and Larry stood to open the door for him.

"See you in the morning."

4

$ $ $

LARRY SAW DAVID CHANCELLOR THE NEXT MORNING, BRIEFLY, as Pat was showing him to her reserved parking space; but he did not see either of them during the rest of the day. He was busy around, in, and out of Campaign Headquarters. Just for the hell of it he played a little innocent footsie with various of the available ones, always leaving the deliberateness of his actions open to question, if that was the way they wanted it, but gaining reassurances of his judgment by their reactions. He found but mild satisfaction in the game, however. Time was running out anyway, and Batesville was not growing any larger or any more tolerant.

He did have dinner with his boss.

"How did you come out?" he asked, after David Chancellor had bowed his white head and mumbled grace in the public dining room.

"Closed four. I am calling on one after dinner this evening, and I have an appointment in the morning."

"Mrs. Bates?" Larry asked. Perhaps the question was in order. It was certainly germane.

"Oh yes, Mrs. Bates. Yes, Larry. I am pleased to report that the dear old lady saw the light." David Chancellor main-

24

tained a perfectly straight face. "All she needed was a little guidance."

"Fifty thousand?"

"Your estimate was valid." The old man nodded. "There will be a delay of a few days, however. She wants to have me draw a cashier's check on a New York bank. As you know, she prefers to attract as little attention as possible to her philanthropy."

So the Anonymous Donor was in the bag.

"About noon Saturday, perhaps?" Larry also kept a straight face.

"Yes. I'm sure I can have the check here by air mail about noon Saturday. I'll send it special delivery to the hotel."

Not a crack in the great stone face, not even a hairline. Chancellor met Larry's gaze as evenly as if the deal were strictly on the level.

David Chancellor cleaned up his assignment neatly before noon the next day, and after a brief prayer session with the assembled workers allowed Pat and Larry to drive him to the airport to catch an afternoon flight back to New York. He modestly declined a going-away escort by the entire committee. He had done his small bit; he would not take them away from their labor of love.

At the air terminal he held Pat's hand in both of his and thanked her for the great help she had given him. Then he turned to Larry.

"Thank you, too, my boy, for relinquishing your claim on her services for this short day and a half," he said. His eyes were mocking as he spoke, and his voice was smug. In the short day and a half he had learned Pat well enough to know that his field hand was making no hay in that meadow. He was gloating behind that pious façade.

"Feel better now?" Pat asked on the way back to town.

"Yes. Mr. Chancellor left us in good shape. It's mostly coasting from here on in."

"I'm getting butterflies, now that we are so near our goal

—a little frightened to think that the new church is so near a reality. It seems too good to be true—I mean such a beautiful church, with such wonderful youth facilities. I've hoped, I've prayed, but somehow—"

" 'O ye of little faith,' " Larry chided her.

"But I do have faith," she insisted seriously. "Still, I've wanted the new building so badly, especially the youth wing. I guess I've been selfish and I know it. Perhaps I feel guilty, wanting material things for my work. Anyway, I've been keeping my fingers crossed and hoping. If we don't make it I'll just die. And if we do—"

"When we do," Larry assured her.

"When we do, I guess I'll just explode with sheer joy and thanksgiving. Do I sound silly?" she asked, suddenly turning to face him.

"Not at all. Devoted, dedicated to your work, just as I would expect you to sound."

"I don't know. Not really." She looked and sounded strange as she spoke. "Maybe you're right, or maybe I'm trying to prove something to myself." Then she brightened, as though deliberately pulling herself back from somewhere. "But that's not your problem. How much more do we need?"

"Not much. Fifty, seventy-five thousand. We'll make it by Saturday easily."

"I hope so. *All* of it. If we don't go over the top, the first alternates to be dropped will be in youth facilities. I couldn't bear that. I just couldn't."

"We'll make it, all of it." Larry tried to sound comforting. "Look at what we've done these last two days."

"Mr. Chancellor *is* wonderful, isn't he?" She might have been speaking of her Blessed Savior.

"Number one in the business," Larry said, trying not to sound bitter. Last week *he* had been the wonderful one. Then Pat had been assigned to help *him*; she had been loyal to *him*. That was the way she was.

26

Her butterflies kept fluttering the next few days. Larry watched her tighten up as the final gleanings dribbled in.

"I was always like this before a ball game in college," she told Larry once when she caught him studying her. "I was a cheerleader, you know, and a physical-ed major. That made ball games a little more personal to me." She laughed nervously.

Larry was somewhat tense himself when Campaign Headquarters closed Saturday noon and the Key Personnel gathered for the final accounting. He was steeling himself for the sticky part.

Brother Hilliard called the meeting to order and asked for the auditor's report. Brother Harris droned through the various categories, raising his voice only slightly when he announced subtotals. Some of these were greeted with expressions of pleasant surprise, and Larry watched the Key Personnel frown and move their lips as they tried to keep a running total in their minds.

"So, I get a grand total"—Brother Harris paused for effect —"of five hundred fifty-three thousand, three hundred forty dollars."

His announcement was greeted by a round of applause —sighs of relief, gasps of surprise at the amount, and smug, self-congratulatory smiles.

"Do your figures agree with mine, Larry?" Brother Harris asked.

"Exactly," Larry said, and nerved himself to enter the unpopularity contest. "I have prepared a report for Mr. Chancellor based on that total. It shows the fifteen-per-cent fee to Christian Benevolences, Inc., to be eighty-three thousand, one hundred eleven dollars, leaving a net to Calvary Church of four hundred seventy thousand, two hundred twenty-nine dollars."

"Yes, Brother Harris. I believe our figures agree."

Larry drew no applause with his financial statement. Instead it was greeted by a stunned silence. Then Larry watched the computers go back into action; the lips started moving

27

again. The fifteen per cent, which as a mere abstraction had passed almost unnoticed in the original discussion around the Round Table in the Home Office, began to loom large when translated into dollars and cents to be deducted from Brother Harris's grand total. The Key Personnel had just realized that a great big helping of that lovely money had to be ladled right off the top and served up to Christian Benevolences, Inc.

"So we are thirty thousand dollars short," Brother Hilliard, Campaign Chairman, observed. His voice sounded hollow, as if it came from the depth of a well.

After the campaign had run so smoothly, too. The people could probably have done just as well without calling in a fund-raising agency. *They* had done the job. Just look at the workers' names on all those pledge cards—names of the congregation, friends soliciting friends, God's own children doing His work in His own church—all in the family. Who was David Chancellor, anyway, to con a gullible congregation out of eighty-three thousand dollars? A mercenary carpetbagger.

The mental processes of the Key Personnel functioned in unison, reached the conclusion simultaneously; and the eyes of the Key Personnel turned on Larry in a single motion. He smiled bravely, hoping for at least one sign of pity on the surly countenances encircling him. He felt like grinning idiotically and saying, "Gee, fellows, I'm only the hired hand." Come to think of it, he probably was grinning idiotically.

The sourest look of all clouded the face of Brother Hilliard. He was the one who would have to report to the congregation at the morning service. And he could not very well complain; it was his committee that had called in Christian Benevolences, Inc., in the first place. He was the first to speak, however.

"Well, I suppose we ought to get together on a report to the congregation, Brother Harris," he said. It was obvious that he wanted no more assistance from Laurence P. Shelton.

No one spoke directly to Larry, but practically everyone made some comment for him to overhear. In the midst of

28

growing hostility, he began to gather up his papers and other things strewn around Campaign Headquarters.

"I'll help you with those," Pat Hayden offered, at his elbow.

"Thanks. This is quite a load."

The two of them carried his stuff out to her car. She was more gracious, but little less glum, than the others.

"I'm sorry," she said on the way to the hotel. "For you, I mean. Those people forgot the money you did help them raise. All they saw was the deficit, the hole in the doughnut."

"And it's your thirty thousand dollars," Larry said, watching her out of the corner of his eye. He hated to make her wait with the others for the delayed manna being held for him by the desk clerk.

"Yes," she said despondently. "But I guess I always knew we wouldn't get everything I wanted for the youth program. As I said, I've been selfish."

"I can't believe you're being punished for wanting something for others. The kids are the ones who are being short-changed."

"That's what hurts. We've planned so much together. Now we'll have to go on making do. If I only had the money myself." She beat on the steering wheel with one clenched fist.

"The world hasn't come to an end," Larry said. "Just the fund drive. Time goes on. There's still money around."

"But not for years. And don't say 'patience' to me," she said, glancing at him and smiling with a spark of her usual good humor.

"I wouldn't think of it."

Pat parked her car in a vacant space a little way from the hotel entrance.

"I'll still help you with those," she said, and they gathered up their bundles and entered the lobby.

They stopped by the desk, where Larry picked up his key and his mail. It was there, all right, the letter from the Home

29

Office. They walked up the stairs and down the long hall of the rambling two-story hotel.

Larry unlocked his door and let Pat precede him into the room. She put her armful of papers down on his desk, then took his folders and started arranging them in neat little stacks.

Larry opened the letter from the Home Office.

"Well, what do you know?" he said in feigned surprise.

"What?" Pat turned to face him.

"A check from Christian Benevolences for a gift by an anonymous donor—fifty thousand dollars!"

"You're kidding, Larry. You're kidding." Her eyes opened wide in disbelief.

"See for yourself." He handed her the letter.

She read it once, then again. "Oh, Larry. It's true. It *is* true! We've made it—*all* of it and then some!"

With the most innocent, ingenuous reflex ever, she flung her arms around his neck and hugged him. He might have been anyone or anything when she first kissed him in her sudden joy. But it was a mistake. What began as a sheer release of long-pent-up anxiety merged into a deep probing kiss. The alchemy of physical contact transmuted her gesture of gratitude, or whatever it was, into a surge of sensual outpouring. Her mouth smothered his. Her breasts strained at his chest. There was no stopping her instincts.

She probably never knew how she got out of her light summer dress and sheer underthings and into his bed. Her actions were not deliberate or intentional, but neither were they inept or inexpert. The honest rhythm of her lithe young hips was the natural response of a physical-ed major.

Larry reveled in a mood of lyricism. Pat treated him to an ecstatic half hour the like of which he would probably never know again, unless he could induce her to change her whole way of life. And as she lay in his arms, allowing herself to be petted back into the state of normalcy expected of a respectable youth director, the latter possibility became progressively more remote. Although he made the most of the moment, he felt himself slipping, losing the will to push to its limit whatever advantage he had gained. In less excited moments surely he would come to scoff at his irrational resolve to keep that one experience unique, inviolate, forever free from profanation. He was not thinking at all like an old field hand; but this was no routine Saturday-afternoon romp.

Pat stirred in his arms. She tensed against his own delicious relaxation.

"I think I'd better go, Larry," she said. "I mustn't compromise you."

Compromise him! She let him kiss her once more, but with no response on her part, and left his bed.

"Look, Pat—" Larry began, when she came out of his bathroom and started dressing herself, solemnly, carefully, quite unself-consciously.

"Don't feel too bad about this, Larry," she said. "Don't think that you've suddenly awakened me or that I've just discovered something wild and evil in myself. I've known about it—always. I've known it was there, but I've been careful. That's the main reason why I joined the Life Recruits and went into church work. I thought I might stay good if I could keep myself fenced in by virtue.

"Well, it didn't work, did it?" She smiled, with an unaccustomed cynicism.

"Now, Pat—" he began.

"It's all right. It had to happen sometime, I suppose. Of course things have changed now, but it's not your fault." She examined her reflection in his mirror and got to his door before he could open it for her.

"Goodbye, Larry," she said. "I'm glad you raised all the money."

"Goodbye, Pat." That was all he could say. He wished he could have told her that fund raising was the messiest part of Christian service—that he should never have let her get mixed up in it—that she was not damned beyond redemption.

He wished he had told her that; but she had left him tongue-tied.

Larry was in no hurry to report the anonymous gift to Brother Hilliard and his finance committee. Let them sweat over their deficit. Let them fret over Chancellor's bite. Let them prepare their report and chew on one another until they were good and sore, until the belated cashier's check would really look like manna from heaven.

He tidied up his papers and filed them in cartons for shipment to the Home Office. Then he opened his laundry and packed it, along with the contents of various closets and drawers, ready for a speedy get-the-hell-out-of-town. He judged that Brother Hilliard was about half through his dinner when he finally decided to break the news.

"What do you want, Shelton?" the good brother asked grumpily when he had been piped to the telephone by a member of his brood.

"I want to make a supplementary report on the fund drive."

"All right, make it."

"I have received, by special delivery, a late check from an anonymous donor."

"For how much?" Brother Hilliard was not impressed.

"For fifty—thousand dollars."

"For how much?" Brother Hilliard *was* impressed—astounded.

"Fifty thousand dollars."

"Fifty thousand! Say, Larry, that's really something, ain't it? Changes the whole picture. When can I—when can we—"

"I thought—in the morning—" Larry already had a ticket for a late coach flight to New York.

"In the morning, nothing. I can get the committee together in thirty minutes. Let me spread the word and meet you at the church in half an hour."

"O.K., if you like."

32

Larry checked out of the hotel and sent his bags to the airport by taxi.

An entirely different set of faces greeted him when he entered Campaign Headquarters. It was "Hi, Larry" all around, and a gauntlet of violent handshakes. He was the fair-haired boy again, and David Chancellor was the good old white-haired Benefactor of all mankind.

Brother Harris retotaled his accounts, and the mere ninety-thousand-six-hundred-eleven-dollar fee to Christian Benevolences, Inc., paled into relative insignificance.

"Say, that leaves us nearly fourteen thousand dollars to the good," Brother Hilliard noted jubilantly.

"Thirteen thousand, seven hundred thirty-nine." Brother Harris tried to remain calm in the face of the figures, as a CPA should.

Each in his own way reacted to the windfall as violently as had Pat Hayden. Hers was the reaction Larry remembered on the night flight to New York.

5

$ $ $

LARRY STAYED ONE DAY AND NIGHT IN THE NEW YORK APART-ment which he shared with his sister and her husband, and then spent his bonus week yawling around Martha's Vineyard,

Woods Hole, and Buzzards Bay with a sea-struck underling from one of the Diseases. The leisurely cruise, a little skin-diving here and there, and the companionable commiseration of a fellow genius stymied by the fat cats upstairs purged him of much of his summer's discontent, so that he was reconciled to greeting David Chancellor with some measure of civility when he reported back to work on the Tuesday after Labor Day.

He was reasonably gay as he entered the respectable old building on Church Street and rode up in the elevator with Carmen, admiring her bosom, which her strenuous tours of duty opening and closing the heavy hand-operated door kept at a wondrous peak of condition, and acknowledging with a smile the shy look of appreciation in her warm Puerto Rican eyes as she turned her face up to his and called, "Eleven, please."

The hall on the eleventh floor was as old-fashioned as the elevator. Plain glass transoms tilted inward above frosted panels in sturdy oak doors which matched the wainscot running the length of the corridor.

He went to the last suite on the left and opened a door modestly labeled CHRISTIAN BENEVOLENCES, INC.

The primmest of all blue-haired receptionists looked up from her desk as he entered.

"Good morning, Miss Mary," he said. "Is God in?"

"Larry Shelton!" Miss Mary was horrified, as usual. "You're blasphemous."

She was already blushing; so Larry's affectionate peck on her cheek did little more than heighten her color. She squeezed his arm, though, even while she was cluck-clucking him to shame.

"Mr. Chancellor is in, yes," Miss Mary said, "and I believe he's expecting you. But I'm not sure I should send you in until you learn to behave."

"How respectful can I get?"

"I wish you'd let your hair grow. Why anyone with such

nice wavy hair would wear a crew cut." Her eyes played fondly over his features.

"You want me to look pretty?"

"Heavens no. You couldn't look pretty." Miss Mary rose, still facing him. "But you were about as handsome as a big ugly boy could be—before you got a crew cut, that is."

"Wigs are all the rage now, I hear. Maybe I'll wear one just for you."

Larry followed her into the general office, a fairly large room where two accountants and several typists were already at work. They all looked up and nodded, but no one spoke.

"I'll check with Miss Julie," Miss Mary said softly. "Wait here." She knocked on a solid door at her right and, after a moment, opened it and disappeared.

Larry ambled over to the typist nearest the rail and said, "Someday I'm going to stomp in here and yell, 'Hello, everybody.' "

"I doubt that," the typist said, and glanced up with an expression as skeptical as her words.

"You've been reading my mail," Larry teased.

"I've been answering your mail," she said without bothering to look up a second time.

"Oh," Larry said, and drifted away from her desk. Something wrong here, he thought.

Miss Mary returned and held the inner door open.

"Miss Julie says you may come in."

"Thanks," Larry said.

Miss Julie, who did not bother to blue her hair, was nevertheless well groomed and well preserved for her age.

"Good morning, Mr. Shelton," she said—no familiarity, no foolishness. "Go right in."

Larry went right in, aware that two heavy oak doors were being closed behind him.

David Chancellor stood behind his desk at the far end of the long office, beyond the Round Table.

"Good morning, Larry," he said, extending his hand across the desk.

"Good morning, sir," Larry said cheerily, beyond the call of mere civility, because something in his Master's voice added vaguely to the unease he had begun to feel in the outer office.

"Sit down, sit down." David Chancellor perfunctorily indicated the chair facing the desk and settled down into his own. "You turned in your usually fine report on the Calvary Church campaign." The same old lyrics, but a brand-new tune.

"Thank you, sir." Larry sat down facing the east windows, through which the bright morning sun caused him to blink before his pupils could make proper adjustment.

"It seems that we overlooked nothing."

"Didn't miss a bet." Larry's civility had limits. The sunlight was too much like a third-degree spot in precinct headquarters.

"I trust that you didn't use that expression during the campaign, my boy. I've warned you once about your language."

"No sir. I was careful during the campaign."

"During the campaign, yes." The old man's hands enacted their pious pantomime below the white piped V, but the voice was taunting. "You rendered valuable service, did an excellent job of counseling those who needed guidance in their giving. You went the second mile with your workers, as you always have in your campaigns."

David Chancellor's eyes got into the act. They began to draw a bead on Larry's face. And behind them was a charge of malice that gravely threatened the accustomed benignity of the great man's countenance.

"Thank you, sir." Larry exhausted his civil reserves.

"Indeed, if the paraphrase is not irreverent, I shall say that you went a third mile." The bead zeroed in. "There was nothing in our agreement which required you to seduce the youth

36

director of Calvary Church—that beautiful little girl who appeared to be so fine and virtuous!"

So that was it. He could resent a first-rate field director who might someday challenge his position as dean of fund raisers and still hold himself in check—that was money in his pocket. He could put up with a little flippancy now and then which might tarnish the Image. But the success of a lusty young field hand in enterprises beyond the reach of his Master's senility was more than he could bear.

"You might call that service extra-contractual," Larry said, grinning.

"I might call it disgraceful, reprehensible, disgusting, and unpardonable." The old man's voice and body trembled as he spoke.

"You might, at that," Larry agreed. He sensed that he was being fired, but by God he was watching the façade of the Heavenly Kingdom shatter into rubble, insofar as it was represented by this saintly satyr.

"You must realize that your career is at an end." David Chancellor was trying to reassume his bishop's manner. "Christian Benevolences has always been above reproach ethically, morally, spiritually—second only to the Church itself in integrity. In despoiling that lovely child, you have defiled, besmirched our good name."

"Who broadcast this heinous crime of mine? Who was peeking?"

"No one was peeking, as you so crudely put it. Your conscience-stricken victim, retaining some shreds of Christian decency even after her fall, considered herself unworthy of her calling. She wanted no hint of another scandal to touch Calvary Church. So she resigned her position and in prayerful supplication with her pastor revealed her sin and named her seducer."

"Poor kid. There was no need."

"Not according to your debased code of morals, perhaps, but by hers—and upon the urging of Dr. Briggs. He, fortunately, has been most discreet and considerate of the welfare of his church and of Christian Benevolences—a truly compassionate man. Only he and I know of the degrading incident. He accepted her resignation and apology, as I shall welcome yours."

"Apology, hell. I quit, period."

"Watch your language, Larry!" Under stress Chancellor's baritone rose into the soprano register. Then, in an embarrassing attempt at self-control, he opened a folder on his desk and nervously fingered the papers on top.

"I've prepared a reckoning. On the Calvary Church campaign, nine thousand, sixty-one dollars and ten cents as your—"

"Tithe," Larry supplied.

"Eight hundred forty dollars and thirty-three cents, as per your itemized expense account. Net salary—after deductions for income tax, OASI, hospitalization, and insurance—twelve hundred sixty-six dollars and eleven cents. Here are three checks, for your convenience." He handed them across the desk to Larry. "You may audit—"

"Never mind," Larry said. "I never knew you to make a financial error." He pocketed the checks without glancing at them.

With a forced attempt at a smile, but with a great deal of malicious satisfaction, David Chancellor said, "I am truly sorry to see so promising a career come to an end."

"To an end?" Larry repeated.

"You can hardly expect to continue in any phase of Christian solicitation. Surely, you must understand that, my boy. We're all one big fraternity, and I consider it my sacred duty—"

"To blackball me?" Larry laughed shortly.

The other man laughed too. "No hard feelings," he said, rising, as Larry stood up, to show him to the door.

"None at all."

"I do wish you every success in whatever other field you

seek employment." David Chancellor came around the end of his desk and shook Larry's hand. He fell into step with him during the walk down the long office and awkwardly laid an arm across Larry's shoulders.

He had never before touched a field hand, to the best of Larry's knowledge. What more could the old bastard want? Whatever it was, it was coming hard.

"Larry," the Master said at last, huskily, "man to man, what was she like?"

If he could have felt any pity for the old goat, Larry might have answered, "Instinctively expert." Instead, he shrugged the arm off his shoulder and burst out laughing.

"You sanctimonious son of a bitch," he said before opening the door into Miss Julie's sentry box.

He was still laughing when he passed through the outer office to Miss Mary's reception desk.

"What on earth are you laughing at?" Miss Mary asked, startled out of her usual composure.

"At the great David Chancellor."

"Oh, no, Larry." She rose hurriedly and ran to grip his arm. "Did he hear you?"

"Yes."

"Goodness gracious! You should never have done that. He can't—he couldn't stand being laughed at. He'll fire you."

"He already has."

Her hands tightened convulsively on his upper arm.

"Then he'll ruin you," she said.

"He promised to do that, too."

"Oh, my!" Miss Mary was terror stricken.

Larry hugged the prim old lady and kissed her scented blue hair. Then he eased her away and let himself out into the wainscoted corridor.

6

$ $ $

KATY, HIS SISTER, WAS OUT WHEN LARRY RETURNED TO THE apartment, but she came in soon after he arrived.

"Home early, I see," she said upon finding him sitting on the sofa smoking a cigarette.

"Yes." He rose to help her with her armload of groceries. She was three years younger than he, with his brown hair and hazel eyes—a little taller than average. Not pretty, but far from unattractive.

"How were things at the mine?" she asked on the way to the kitchen.

"Best ever. I quit."

"You what?" She set her bag of groceries on the drainboard and stared at him in surprise.

"Quit," he repeated, putting down his load.

"Shall I ask why?"

"I wouldn't."

"O.K., I won't, but I'll guess. I guess you got fed up with chancellor of the holy exchequer. You've never made a secret of your feelings toward His Holiness." She began taking her purchases out of the bags and storing them away.

"That's a fair guess."

"What'll you do now?"

40

"I'm not sure, maybe nothing for a while. It's the slack season in Christian benevolences anyway. The Community Chest and United Fund drives are just kicking off, and pretty soon the Diseases will take over again full time. You know the calendar."

"No. Frankly, I don't. Brief me."

"O.K. January: Cerebral Palsy and the March of Dimes. February: Heart. March: Leukemia, the Red Cross, and Crippled Children. April: Cancer and Myasthenia Gravis. May: Mental Health and Multiple Sclerosis. Then the money hunters go fishing but return for Arthritis and Rheumatism in September, Muscular Distrophy in October, Retarded Children in November, and Tuberculosis for Christmas." Larry ticked the campaigns off on his fingers and then counted his eyes, ears, and nose.

"Really, Larry! You're kidding. There aren't that many fund drives."

"Indeed, there are."

"Of course we buy a ticket to some charity function now and then, and Christmas seals, and there are all those pesky things in the mail; but I had no idea—"

"That's the way with you quaint villagers on the coastal islands—Staten, Manhattan, and Long. You have no idea of the continuous pressure the fund raisers put on the average mainlander. His doorbell is ringing constantly. Thousands of local volunteers always putting the bite on him. And these are only the Diseases. Think of the local projects, churches—. Have you ever contributed to a church drive, Sis?"

"Well, no. We already have churches in New York City."

"Exactly. You already have everything. Hospitals, churches, parks. You have always had everything. You are self-sufficient."

"Are you hinting that we islanders are a mite provincial? Those are the attitudes of a stagnant provincialism, I hear."

"Not at all. I'm merely saying that you don't know, and presumably don't care, what goes on west of the Hudson. I do. I work there. Believe me, there are as many money hunters in the hinterland as there are muggers and pushers in the city."

"Oh, dear. And you are one of those obnoxious creatures yourself. I can remember when you were quite nice, and happy in your work. And now you aren't even working. What will you do?"

"I think I'll just loaf until the NAFR pep rally in October—I should be able to latch onto something at the convention." Unless David Chancellor was able to keep the blackball rolling.

"Oh, sure. How many months do you usually loaf around—about six a year?"

"Let's say I'm a seasonal worker."

"And it's closed season. What do you want for lunch?"

Katy brewed coffee and made salads for both of them while he was foraging. Then they ate together in the kitchen.

He got along fine with Katy, and with her husband, Herb Phillips, who was about his age, a rising junior partner in a midtown law firm; but basically he was not a house cat. Katy's reference to his loafing around was of course an exaggeration. David Chancellor had always kept him busy between fund drives, even if the jobs were sometimes make-work. Real loafing might come hard.

As he reviewed his acquaintanceship in NAFR, Larry could think of a number of fair possibilities. There was no reason for him to panic. He had already made over fifty thousand dollars that year; so he was solvent, even after the IRS bite. He could spare a month or so, but one did not move freely in and out of the money-hunting racket. One who loafed too long was a has-been.

The first thing a has-been knew he was working for peanuts in a Community Chest or United Fund setup somewhere, or combining public relations and fund raising in a jerkwater college for room and board. Laurence P. Shelton was certainly above that sort of thing.

He was watching TV when Herb came in.

"Hi, Larry," Herb greeted him. "I hear you've parted company with Christian Benevolences."

"News travels fast."

"Miss Mary called me at the office. She was worried to the brink of a migraine."

"Bless her old heart," Larry said fondly.

"You may well bless her heart, you no-good bastard. If you're in trouble and need money, now that you've quit your job—I'll bet you were fired—she has a little nest egg saved up. But I'm to help you out and not let you know where the money comes from. You don't deserve a gal like Miss Mary."

"Oh, I don't know."

"I do. And I've always known I'd have a shiftless brother-in-law. Everybody has." He threw the evening paper at Larry and went off toward the kitchen to interrupt Katy's pan-rattling.

Not a bad home life. Not bad at all, but it began to pall on Larry within a week. The second Sunday he found himself reading the want ads. He was relapsing into the near panic he had felt upon his release from the navy after a two-year hitch supporting the occupation forces in Korea. He slammed the classified section shut and forced himself to reread the front page.

The lead story was a sensational account of a policeman who had been stabbed to death by a gang of teenage boys in the hallway of a West Side tenement house. He scanned the straight news story, then desultorily turned to the human-interest feature bemoaning the pitiable plight of the officer's bereft widow and two fatherless sons, ages three and four. Next he turned to an editorial which decried the delinquency of the younger generation, the inadequacy of the police pension program, the general apathy of the entire city toward crimes of violence, and growing disrespect for law and order everywhere.

Too bad, Larry thought complacently. And then *too bad* —too bad, indeed!—too bad about that poor widow and those two helpless little boys. Somebody ought to do something about it, somebody who had time on his hands, somebody who was trying to loaf for a month or so, somebody who ought to be keeping his hand in.

He returned to the lead story and found the dead policeman's address. Then he put on a coat and tie, hurried downstairs, and hailed a taxi. On the way across town his mind raced. He thought of a dozen plans for a campaign, reviewed them, rejected them, recalled them, and re-examined them. One kept returning, but it was a ticklish one, a slightly indelicate one which would have to be approached with extreme delicacy. He would have to wait until he saw the widow. If she were amenable it would work.

As the taxi bucked traffic and nosed into Tenth Avenue, Larry straightened up in his seat, unconsciously fingered the knot in his tie, and began to induce a somber mood. He was feeling like an apprentice undertaker by the time the driver located Officer Burke's address. The building had been recently renovated, but it looked little better than the picture of the tenement house in which the stabbing had taken place.

Larry found Officer Burke's name on a mailbox and made his way to Widow Burke's apartment. He fingered his tie again, straightened his face, and pushed the button below the molded plastic numerals. Nothing happened. He punched again. Not a sound. The bell must have been out of order. He knocked on the door, softly—only, it was a hollow plywood slab which responded like a tom-tom. His presence was known.

He still heard no other sound, and was about to knock again when the door opened halfway and slowly revealed the whitest face, the bluest eyes, the reddest mouth, and the blackest hair he had ever seen in combination.

"Mrs. Burke?" he asked, a little tardily, allowing a moment for recovery from the immediate shock of her blatant beauty.

"Yes?"

44

"I'm Laurence P. Shelton. May I come in for a minute?"

"Oh, yes. Sure. Come in." She opened the door wider and appeared full-figure—literally—in a loose sleeveless wrapper casually held together at the neck by her left hand. "I was lying down. They said I should. Widows always do."

"I'm sorry to have awakened you."

"It's all right. Sit down." She indicated a chintz-covered sofa.

She sat on one end of the sofa and Larry on the other. She looked at him appraisingly, but waited for him to state his business.

"I wanted to talk to you about the boys. About taking care of them."

"Mrs. Burke—Pat's mother—has them. She's taking care of them. She don't like me." Mrs. Burke—Pat's widow—seemed inclined to give a little more information than was being sought. Indeed, as she relaxed her grip on the wrapper Larry noted that she had a little bit more of everything than was absolutely necessary, but it was a becoming surplus.

"I don't mean right now. I mean in the future," he explained.

"Are you trying to sell me some kind of insurance?"

"No." Larry decided to be as forthright as Widow Burke. "No, Mrs. Burke, I'm not trying to sell you anything. I am a fund raiser. Members of my profession are always raising money for widows and orphans. I'd like to try to do something for you and your boys. Moneywise, that is."

"How much?" She was waking up.

"A hundred thousand dollars, two hundred thousand. It all depends."

"That much?" She was wide awake.

"It's been done."

"How?"

"We'll have to work out a campaign. That's what I came to talk about. I have an idea. You may not like all of it, but it might go over big."

"Shoot."

"Well, I have in mind a fund for the Sons of the Brave. Your husband, their father, was a brave man. He risked his life for all the little boys in New York City. I think the people of New York might appreciate it. They might want to repay some of their debt—to his sons."

"They might." She smiled enigmatically, revealing even white teeth which heightened the already astonishing contrasts in her face. Slavic ancestry, he guessed.

"But—and this is the ticklish part—I might want to add a little fillip." He felt that he was on reasonably firm ground. "I might want to refer to your children as the little s.o.b.'s sometimes."

"I don't know what a fillip is, Mister, but for a hundred grand you can refer to my children as 'the little s.o.b.'s' any time you want to. Their father was a big S.O.B., an honest to God son of a bitch—the real McCoy." Her smile was a little twisted.

"Then, it's a deal, Mrs. Burke?"

"It's a deal. Call me Eileen."

"O.K., Eileen. Do you have a lawyer?" Larry was loath to call Herb in as the attorney.

"Pat knew some mouthpieces. I'll see one of them at the funeral tomorrow."

"Fine, you arrange for us to get together and draw up a contract—as soon as possible, while this case is still in the news."

"What do you expect to get out of this. Mr.—er—?" She paused for a first name.

"Larry."

"Larry."

"Fifteen per cent."

"Sounds about right, Larry. Here's my hand on it." She stood up, making no attempt to rewrap the wrapper.

Larry took her hand, soft of texture but bold and firm in its grip.

"I wish to God we could drink to it, but Mrs. Burke —Pat's mother—may bring the boys back here any minute."

"Some other time," Larry suggested.

"Some other time for sure." The red, white, blue, and black dazzled him again and managed to brush against him ever so lightly on the way to the door.

Out in the street again, he revised some of his ideas about pictures for the campaign. The little boys might look winsome and helpless enough, but one publicized shot of their voluptuous mother would stall a fund drive before the gears were meshed. He just might have taken on a bigger job than he could handle.

7

$ $ $

THE DAY AFTER THE FUNERAL, EILEEN BURKE CALLED UP LARRY and asked him to meet her at her lawyer's office, which turned out to be a grubby little cubicle in a building occupied mostly by bail-bond brokers. Barrister Fenton was a beady-eyed, hatchet-faced fixture small enough and grubby enough to have been designed expressly for the room he adorned.

Eileen Burke was something else, again. Her weeds were black all right, but they might have been designed by the couturier for the Big Wheel. She could have worn that sheath and veil and those long black gloves across any burlesque stage in the land and immediately raised the chant, "Take it off, take it off." At that, she would have been stunning at an uptown cocktail party.

"Hi, Larry," she said eagerly. "I've told Springer what we had in mind. He's already drawn up a rough draft."

"Yeah, Eileen sort of outlined it for me. I think I got the drift all right."

Larry read through the yellow sheets with growing admiration. David Chancellor's legal counsel could not have done better. "Springer" Fenton had anticipated every possible loophole and plugged it neatly and effectively. His documents would stand up in the courts, in the State of New York, and in the skeptical eyes of the Internal Revenue Service.

"Looks good to me," Larry commented.

"Yeah, when Eileen approached me, I figured she had latched on to a sharpie. Used to be with Chancellor's outfit, I understand. That's good enough for me, and I told Eileen so. I saw right away that you and I could do a lot for this little girl and her two fine boys. So I took her case on a contingency basis."

"Contingency basis?"

"Yeah, ten per cent of the gross. She won't owe me a penny if it don't work out."

"That's fine with me, Larry," Eileen agreed happily.

"Then I'm sure I have no objections. Fix up the final draft, Counselor, and I'll go along with the contract as written." What Eileen did with the money was her business. With her legal adviser, she would probably do very well.

Larry went back across town to Herb's office and started his brother-in-law to work on the papers which would make Laurence P. Shelton Associates, Community Funds Consultants, stand up as well as Springer Fenton's contracts. He had to confide his plans to Herb, who he hoped would consider them privileged communications between attorney and client. Larry was a little shamefaced until Herb began kidding him.

"You might be rendering a genuinely humanitarian service, you know," Herb said. "The little s.o.b.'s could have pretty hard sledding later on if someone didn't take an interest in them, be he bastardly or benevolent."

"Or both," Larry suggested.

"I'll leave it open. Anyway, I hope it keeps you busy. I hate having an unemployed relative around the house."

"By the way," Larry said, "if Miss Mary calls again you may tell her that I am up to my neck in solvency. Tell her I am working—*but* no more."

"Won't she wonder?" Herb asked.

"Sure. So will David Chancellor. That's one of the things I have in mind. I'd like for Christian Benevolences to wonder what I'm doing." Larry grinned and left Herb to attend to his legal affairs.

Actually, Larry wondered if his chief aim in the whole plan was not to thumb his nose at Christian Benevolences. If so, he had certainly made a promising choice of subject in that he could make his gesture a broad one, from the sublime to the obscene.

He began his campaign gently enough, by planting an appealing picture of the tots—no mama in sight—in a sob story which he peddled, flattered, and cocktailed to three sentimental newshens of his acquaintance. He followed up the very next day with sizable advertisements featuring the same pictures and announcing the *Fund for the Sons of the Brave.* His simple plea was:

If you
CARE
what happens to these little
Sons of the Brave
send your contribution to
P.O. Box 1776C
Mount Vernon, New York

The first response to his advertisements came as a knock on his apartment door, which he opened to find very well filled by a burly Irishman, obviously a cop in plain clothes.

"Are you Laurence P. Shelton?" his caller asked.

"Yes."

"Inspector Meredith wants to see you over at precinct headquarters." The detective flashed his credentials.

"Am I under arrest? What for?"

"No, Mr. Shelton. Inspector Meredith is just *asking* you over for a talk."

"What about?"

"I don't know, sir, but he wants to talk to you. He'd appreciate it if you came with me."

"Very well. Let me put on a tie and coat." Larry had never been picked up before.

He did not invite his guest in, but his guest came in— all the way into the bedroom—and watched while Larry dressed for his appointment.

"I got a car downstairs," he said as he followed Larry to the elevator.

The police car, unmarked, was waiting at the curb, with another detective at the wheel. Larry and his escort got into the back seat.

"I don't suppose you could give me a hint as to what this is all about," Larry suggested again as the car pulled out into traffic. "I'd like to know what I'm charged with."

"You ain't charged with nothing, so far as I know. I'd say the inspector wanted a friendly chat with you, Mr. Shelton."

"And I suppose that's about all you'd say," Larry said with a smile, trying to keep it friendly.

"About all," the plain-clothes man agreed. If it was to be a friendly chat, Inspector Meredith would have to prove more genial than his underlings, because Larry was not favored with another word or smile until the car stopped behind the late Officer Burke's precinct headquarters.

Springer Fenton would have been—and probably had been—perfectly at home in Inspector Meredith's office, where

50

Larry had to wait in solitary for ten minutes before his inquisitor arrived.

"So you're Shelton," the inspector, a big, muscular specimen, said by way of greeting.

"Yes, Inspector."

"I was sure I'd never seen you." The big man crowded into the chair behind his desk and appraised Larry with imperturbable gray eyes. "Or heard of you. We have nothing on you in the files."

"Well, I'm glad to hear that." Larry tried to establish the friendly basis.

"Yet," Inspector Meredith added. "Just what the hell are you up to, Shelton?" He spread one of the Sons of the Brave ads before Larry.

"Oh, that," Larry said. "I think the appeal is self-explanatory. I'm trying to do something for Patrick Burke's widow and orphans."

"Nuts. How well do you know Eileen Burke?"

"Not at all well. I've seen her three or four times—with her lawyer—to take pictures of the boys—strictly a business acquaintance."

"Yeah. And Springer Fenton?" Meredith spoke Springer Fenton's language.

"About the same. Even less."

"Yeah. There's less of him." But no humor lighted up the inspector's face. "Are you on the level?"

"Absolutely. But I suppose you've checked on me. I've been in the benevolences business for several years. I'm simply interested in humanitarian enterprises."

"Yeah. I've talked to Eileen, and I've read the contracts Springer drew up. Well, you can drop this humanitarian enterprise."

"I don't see why, or how, once it has started rolling. And it has."

Inspector Meredith put the clipping back into a folder and frowned thoughtfully before going on.

"As I say, you're clean with us so far," he began slowly. "But I judge a man by the company he keeps. Not that I have any evidence that you've been keeping company with Eileen Burke." He allowed some of the grimness to go out of his countenance. "Or with Fenton. I suppose you know he's the chief springer for the minor mobsters in this precinct?"

"No, sir, I didn't."

"That's how he got his nickname. Possibly there's a lot more you don't know about this case."

"Possibly," Larry agreed.

"Then I'll give you a few reasons why you ought to call off your dogs. First, this kid—Tony Giachino—who knifed Burke. His mother is the precinct punchboard, and Burke—"

Larry showed his surprise.

"Yeah. You're wondering why Pat would stay out nights, with a babe like Eileen at home. Well, it seems that she turned his water off and on. So he switched for variety. The kids knew about it. They made life hell for young Tony, egged him on to eviscerate Burke—yeah, that's what he had in mind.

"Tony's not a bad kid, but he got into bad company— like you, Shelton—and he ended up killing Burke while some of the other boys held him. So, you see, we don't want to push this case too hard."

"But Burke's little boys are innocent. They're the ones I'm interested in."

"Yeah. And they're two more reasons why you've got to halt your drive. Every cop that's killed in this man's town leaves innocent kids behind. We take care of our own." Meredith fished a cigar out of his breast pocket and stuck it between his teeth.

"Not very well, according to the papers," Larry commented.

Meredith's eyes were not imperturbable after all. They outblazed the match the inspector was putting to his cigar.

"According to the papers! By God, we do the best we can; and you'll louse up what we *are* doing if you start launch-

52

ing a fund drive for the survivors of every cop killed in the city of New York.

"You'll sap the support of our pension plan, PAL, and every other fund we operate. We know what the traffic will bear in this town, and we're pushing it to the limit. We can't have amateurs bollixing up what we've built over the years."

"Amateurs?" Larry was nicked where it hurt.

"O.K., professionals. We deal with professionals of all kinds." Meredith's voice was ominous. "Call off your god-damned dogs, Shelton."

"And publish notices asking people not to support the Sons of the Brave campaign? At the request of the Police Department?" Larry would show him how professionals operated. "Return all contributions received so far—with reasons why? Do you want to sign the order, Inspector Meredith?"

The inspector was as surprised at Larry's flare-up as Larry was himself. He struck another match for his cigar, but he cooled off as the flame burned hotter.

"You're clean with us so far, Shelton," he said in cold, flat tones. "But, by God, we'll watch you from here on. We'll inspect your wiring, your gas connections, your hot-water pipes, your automobile."

"I haven't got an automobile."

"We'll find something. We'll stop this campaign if we can, and we'll head off your next one before it gets started. We'll find ways. Now, get out of here. You're a suspicious character. Remember that."

"I told you I haven't got an automobile."

"What do you mean by that?"

"I want transportation back across town. You sent for me. Send me home." While he was thumbing his nose he might as well make it a broad gesture.

"I'll be god-damned," Inspector Meredith exploded, buzzing an escort for Laurence P. Shelton, suspicious character.

8

$ $ $

THE RESPONSE TO THE CAMPAIGN WAS MODEST AT FIRST, BUT enough mail came into the Mount Vernon box to keep the ads running until everyone knew who the Sons of the Brave were and recognized their pictures on sight. Then Larry added the fillip, on car cards in all the subway trains, posters all over town, and as many money cans as he could place around on cashiers' counters. He modified his appeal to present individual pictures of the winsome little fellows and the text:

If you
CARE
what happens to the little
s.o.b.'s*
mail your contribution to
* Sons of the Brave
P.O. Box 1776C
Mount Vernon, New York

Then he sat back and watched. He had fired his second barrel of scatter shot. Some people were outraged, some amused. The newspapers were divided. One was horrified. Another regretted the breach of good taste, but saw no reason

54

why the vulgarly maligned orphans should have to suffer because of the crude effrontery of their sponsors. The third went along with the gag. But nobody could ignore the campaign, and money poured into the Mount Vernon mailbox. The money cans filled up, sometimes twice a day, especially those placed beside bartenders' cash registers.

Aside from the repeated inspections of the apartment, which infuriated Katy, Larry went through the drive without further police interference. Springer Fenton kept in constant touch by telephone, warning Larry ahead of time of possible snares or slip-ups.

"We pulled it off," Fenton said jubilantly when the campaign was over. "But I'm afraid it was a one-time caper. Meredith is fuming, and the entire force is gunning for you. As much as I would like to collaborate with you on continued operations, I'm afraid I have to advise you to pull in your horns, Shelton."

"Thanks," Larry said. "It was just an interim pastime— a sort of unemployment-relief project."

"Yeah." Springer Fenton chuckled on his end of the line.

The audit showed a gross of three hundred thousand dollars: forty-five thousand for Larry, thirty thousand for Fenton, seventy-five thousand for expenses—a hundred and fifty thousand net, of which a hundred thousand went into a trust fund for the Sons of the Brave and fifty thousand into a drawing account, with their mother as guardian.

Eileen put the boys in a private nursery and kindergarten and moved into a new apartment. She invited Larry over for a housewarming—in the middle of the day.

"I figured we could warm it up," she explained when he arrived and found that he was the only guest.

She had already raised the temperature by appearing in an expensive black negligee sheer enough to leave no doubt that the skimpy garments underneath it were equally chic.

"It's nice," Larry said, forcing his eyes to glance around

55

the apartment—a modern mediocrity which Eileen had not yet lived in long enough to render any less tasteful.

"Glad you like it, Larry. I have the kind of Scotch you like, too." She mixed drinks and invited him to join her on the divan.

She never pushed. She was just there—*all* there—white and black and red and blue. Her eyelashes were real, too, but they did not do any unnecessary tricks. She had so much to offer that there was no need to use it—just display it, as she did while she mixed drinks and brought them back to the divan.

"I appreciate what you've done for me and the boys, Larry," she said.

"I'm glad that I was able to make good my promise. We came out all right."

"I thought you might want more than the fifteen per cent," she said.

"That was our agreement, my usual fee. It's all the money I wanted." He emphasized *money* just enough to evoke the smile he expected. She was there.

And she stayed there—for a few more minutes, until they finished their drinks and Larry moved close enough to taste that startling red mouth. Then they moved into the bedroom, where he learned that her entire body was as white as her face and neck and arms.

Eileen was passive at first, as though she knew what she was like and it was up to him to find out. As he found out, she gradually turned it on, and he could see how her turning it off might have driven Patrick Burke to seek variety, as Inspector Meredith had put it—or in sheer anger and frustration, as was more likely the case. To have her at home, white and passive, but turned off, would have been enough to drive Pat to his death—or worse—under Tony Giachino's knife.

She kept turning it on and off until well into the afternoon, until both were virtually exhausted.

"Can't we do it again, Larry?" she asked after Larry thought it was all over.

He turned over on his side to kiss her. He might manage it, once more.

"I mean the fund drive, silly," she said, and pushed him away playfully. "We still have the boys, and you know how. Couldn't we keep it up?"

"I'm afraid not, Eileen," he said. "Springer says it has to be a one-shot deal."

"We don't need Springer any more."

"He's closer to the police than I am—a lot closer than I ever want to be—and that's what he says."

"Then you agree with him that it's a one-shot deal?"

"Yes, Eileen, I'm afraid I do."

"O.K., so it's a one-shot deal." Symbolically, she got out of bed and starting putting her underthings on.

Larry picked up the cue. He, too, rose silently and started dressing. Neither of them spoke until they were fully clothed —she in considerably more than she had worn to her house-warming party.

"It's been fun," Larry said as she let him out of her apartment.

"Too bad it couldn't last." She gave him the taunting smile which must have sent Officer Burke on his way to Teresa Giachino, and the shiv.

Well, she was not sending Larry Shelton out to be killed by any young punk for the honor of his family. He shuddered as he walked down the hall. In memory Eileen Burke was not the vision of irresistible contrasts she had been in the flesh. She was like Christian Benevolences, Inc., celestially white, radiant in repose, but commercial to the core.

At that she was the peer of Laurence P. Shelton, money hunter de luxe. On the street he kept walking, ignoring the cruising taxis. After a time he found himself headed toward the office of Springer Fenton—seeking his own kind, a vulture returning to its vomit. Or was it because he had business with the little shyster? He did have business with him. Fenton was an associate of his.

The lawyer's office was grubbier than ever, but Larry felt more at home in it. He made himself admit that fact during the few minutes it took him and Springer Fenton to wind up their affairs.

"What's next, boy?" Fenton asked him as he rose to leave.

"I don't know. As you say, this was a one-time caper. I won't try it again."

"You may never pull this one again, but you'll cook up its twin. You've got the old repeater's manner about you, boy."

Larry shook the proffered hand and found himself wiping his own when he left the office. But he was only wiping it on himself.

Back in the apartment, Katy greeted him with obviously forced cordiality.

"All through?" she asked.

"All through."

"What was the widow like? I notice that you didn't feature her in your campaign, and I don't remember having seen her picture."

"So-so. Just a cop's wife. You know, shy, retiring, dowdy. Keeping out of the limelight."

"But grateful."

"Grateful."

"How much did she net on the campaign?"

"A hundred and fifty thousand."

"Out of three hundred thousand?" Katy raised her eyebrows. "Enough to make a widow grateful, but isn't it a little thin? I mean split down the middle? Is that customary?"

"Expenses were heavy," Larry answered defensively. "But did you ever analyze the gross-net ratio of Heart or Cancer?"

"No," Katy admitted. "Should I?"

"It might be enlightening."

"I'm not pushing, Big Brother." Katy eased off. "Where do you go from here?"

"Down to Briarcliff, I suppose." The response was a reflex. He had made no definite plans before that moment. "I think I'll go pack right now."

"The convention doesn't start until the week end."

"I know, but a few days down there, in the mountains, might do me good."

"It might at that." There was relief in her voice in spite of her attempt to conceal it.

So he packed his bags, took a taxi down to Thirty-eighth Street, and a limousine from there to Idlewild. But once at the airport, he called Mrs. Durham in Batesville and found out where Pat was—at home in a small town in southern Ohio. Instead of a ticket to Roanoke, he bought one for a flight to Columbus.

9

$ $ $

LARRY ARRIVED IN COLUMBUS LATE AND SPENT THE NIGHT THERE. The next morning he rented a car and started driving south on Highway 23.

He slow-cruised at a pace that must have been maddening to other drivers in a hurry, but he was still wondering just why he was going to see Pat Hayden and what he was going to say when he did see her. If he was running away from Eileen Burke and her little s.o.b.'s, he was not seeking solace in a precinct punchboard. He was not sure that Pat would even see him. Yes, he was, too. He was sure that she would see him. Then what?

Chillicothe was upon him before he realized it. He checked his map and turned off on a secondary road. He had a very few minutes left. He had stalled about as long as he could. He considered several approaches. He was already driving down Main Street. He could tour the whole town in ten minutes. Pretty soon—

He found Pat's street easily enough, and her house—a comfortable old white frame, freshly painted, set back in an immaculately kept lawn. He drove by and returned to Main Street, where he found a telephone booth.

Pat answered his call.

"This is Larry, Larry Shelton," he said.

"Oh, Larry. How wonderful! What are you doing here?" She sounded cordial enough.

"I was just driving through. I thought I'd call you up, maybe drop by for a few minutes."

"Please do. Where are you?"

"At"—he looked out at a sign—"at Hammond's service station. In a phone booth."

She was standing on the front porch when he turned into the driveway, but she did not rush out to meet him. She wore a simple house dress, but what she did for it would have put in on the cover of any homelife magazine.

"It's so good to see you," she said. "Do come in. I want you to meet Mama."

Mrs. Hayden was a handsome, capable-looking woman in her late forties, as well kept as her house and lawn.

"Mama, this is Larry Shelton. I met him while I was working in Batesville."

Larry was pleased that Pat had not said more, and relieved when her mother did not include "Pat has told me so much about you" in her acknowledgment of the introduction.

"How have you been?" Pat asked after they were alone in the living room.

"Oh, fine. And you?"

"Fine. What have you been doing?"

"A policeman was killed in New York. He left a wife and two little boys. I helped raise funds for their education."

"How wonderful! But I didn't know that Christian Benevolences—Mr. Chancellor—"

"I don't work for Christian Benevolences any more."

"Oh." Pat's face fell. "Larry, it's not—"

"Look, Pat," Larry interrupted. "I want to talk to you —all afternoon. What does one do here? Where can we go to talk?"

"We—we could go bowling," she suggested. "That is, if you have something casual to wear."

"I do. I'm on my way to Briarcliff. You know, the resort in West Virginia."

"Good. You can change at the bowling alley—or won't you spend the night with us? We have plenty of room. You can just go upstairs and—"

"No. I couldn't do that. I'll drive on to Charleston tonight."

"O.K.," she said, rising. "Wait here while I change."

She disappeared into the hall, and Larry heard her going back to tell her mother where she would be. In a few minutes she returned, wearing stretch pants and a sweater, and carrying her bowling ball in a leather bag. She was the girl stretch pants and sweaters had been designed for.

After they were in the car, she asked. "It wasn't on account of me that you left Christian Benevolences, was it, Larry?"

"Of course not." He started the engine.

"It was, too. I know it was. Believe me, Larry. I didn't mean to be a tattletale, really, I didn't. But I *had* to resign, and

I *had* to explain why, and well, Dr. Briggs— But I didn't *want* to involve you. Now, look what I've done to you!"

"Don't be absurd," Larry said a little gruffly. It was not what she had done to him. It was what she was doing to him. "I quit Mr. Chancellor. I've made as much this last month on my own as I had made all year with Christian Benevolences."

"I'm glad. But I'm still to blame."

"What are you doing? What are you going to do? What have I done to you? Those are the questions, the valid ones."

But they had reached the bowling alley. Larry got a bag out of the trunk, and Pat showed him to the men's dressing room, where he changed into slacks and a sport shirt and rented bowling shoes.

"I've reserved us a lane," Pat said when he rejoined her. "It'll be a few minutes. Today is ladies' day—the Homemakers' League."

The place was not crowded, just six teams of dumpy matrons guiltily working off their fat. They all knew Pat. They waved to her, called to her, and probably hated her insides because of her gorgeous outsides.

She and Larry sat on a chromium-and-vinyl settee and waited for the one lane which was not devoted to league play. The clatter of balls and pins covered their conversation.

"Now back to the big question," Larry reminded her.

"Well, I'm not doing anything, right now. The job in Batesville was the only one I ever had. I can't very well ask Dr. Briggs for a recommendation—and—" Everything about Pat was in just proportion except her conscience. "I thought of going into nursing—I want to do something worthwhile—but that means I'll have to go back to school, and the semester has already started. I'll have to wait until mid-term—February."

"And you're the gal who thinks she's loused up my life." Larry laughed mirthlessly. "Pat, you've let things get out of perspective."

"Perspective is the way you look at things," Pat said simply. "That's how I look at me."

"I didn't mean to belittle your—our experience, Pat. It's too—too precious." By God, he believed it. "But you can't—"

"We can bowl now," she said, interrupting him.

Larry bowled just well enough to keep from marring the maple. Pat seemed expert to him, as he had expected her to be. She was expert at anything physical. She kept score, though Larry could very well have kept his own—his squares were not at all cluttered up with strikes and spares.

There talk was mostly about the game, with a remembered incident now and then which they could laugh at, something light they had shared in Batesville. Larry was free to watch Pat in motion, a gradual joy which grew as the afternoon waned.

The Homemakers watched Pat too, but doubtlessly with less personal satisfaction than Larry. As the various teams ended their matches, they paid more attention to Pat's game than to league play.

One of the bolder ones not too hell-and-gone far beyond Pat's age and measurements stood behind Larry and read the score over his shoulder.

"I see you're way off your game today, Pat," she said when Larry rose for his turn.

"Have you read his score?" Pat asked. "I'm way ahead."

"I can understand his distraction," Lena said enviously. "No wonder you've never mentioned him."

"You mean you haven't told Lena about me?" Larry teased, when they were introduced.

"Not a word," Lena answered for Pat. "It's like her bowling. She never puts out any more than she has to win a frame, do you, Pat?"

And when Larry made a strike, his first, Lena was ready with comment. "See? I'm good for your game, Larry. You should be playing with me instead of Miss Freeze-out here."

Larry understood her, and she him. And they both knew Pat. Yes, Lena was one of the ones. If she ever worked on a fund drive with him—he felt a return of the sense of guilt which had brought him to Pat, and which she and her idea of afternoon fun had all but dispelled.

Larry's game sank back into its usual mediocrity, and Pat took her turn. Both of the others watched her breasts point up on her backswing, and her stretch pants stretch as she knelt to release the ball.

Lena took advantage of the ensuing rumble to say, "She'd be worth the chase, Larry; but believe me, you'll have to have a license." With taunting eyes, she turned and walked away from their lane. Larry did not bother to watch what Lena was offering him. One look at Pat had restored his virtue.

"Had enough?" Pat asked, extending their scores.

"Have you?"

"Oh, I could bowl all night," she said, intent on her totals. Larry believed her. And she would enjoy it.

"I guess I've had enough," he said.

"Want to see the scores?"

"I couldn't bear it," Larry said, laughing. "Lady, you've clobbered me."

A cold shower did not chill his emotions. Larry was frightened. He stalled, taking twice the time he needed to dress. He closed his bag and walked out of the locker room carrying his sport clothes over his arm.

Pat was waiting in the car, bowling ball in her lap. She had not gone away, as he had half hoped she might.

Larry started the engine. "So you haven't talked about this wonderful man." He tried to keep it light. "I'm un-flattered."

"I haven't mentioned your name, Larry," she said seriously. "I never thought I'd see you again. I haven't talked much about Batesville. I haven't had to explain anything here —at home—anywhere. I *had* to talk about you to Dr. Briggs, but I won't ever have to tell anyone else I ever knew you, except—"

Oh, sure, she would have to tell her husband. She was like

that. Her husband! The thought was maddening. Her very nearness was maddening, the scent of her beside him.

"Pat, will you marry me?" He blurted it out involuntarily.

"What?" Pat stared at him in surprise. He was being given a chance to retract.

"Marry me." He blew his chance.

"Are you serious?"

"Deadly serious."

"Of course not. I couldn't marry you, Larry. I'd never know—you may feel sorry for me, responsible, gallant, remorseful. No, no, Larry. Don't ask me. You don't owe me a thing."

"Owe you!" He laughed bitterly. "If I thought I owed you something, I'd be offering a hell of a payment. Me."

"Don't unflatter yourself, Larry. You're wonderful—fine. Your proposal proves that. And talented, and successful—"

"And unacceptable."

"Oh, no. I'm happy that you asked me. Thank you, Larry. But you mustn't. It isn't you. It's me." She squeezed his arm once, suddenly, as though pleading with him, and then let go.

He turned into the Hayden driveway.

"Won't you stay for supper?"

"No. I must be getting on."

"You will come in. Daddy will be home."

"No. Really, I can't."

"Forgive me, Larry," she said. "I hope I haven't hurt you—again."

10

$ $ $

THE NEXT MORNING LARRY WOKE UP SORE ALL OVER. HE LAY IN bed awhile, finding some pleasure in the pain of turning over and stretching his muscles and lounging about lazily. Soreness resulting from good honest exercise carried a virtuous relish with it. Still, he was not sure that he wanted to make a career of bowling.

He drove the winding hundred miles through the mountains to Briarcliff before lunchtime. NAFR had held conventions there before, and Larry loved the old place.

Briarcliff was a massive old white brick Georgian structure modeled upon an ante-bellum plantation house with slaves' quarters in the rear, the slaves' quarters being fantastically expensive individual cottages that would have been called cabañas if Briarcliff had been built during the tropical invasion of resort hotels. But then Briarcliff would probably have been named the Capri or the Sahara by latter-day hosts.

He parked at the entrance of the main hotel. The place was all but deserted—would probably close for the year as soon as NAFR had come and gone. Larry was inside at the reservations desk before anyone noticed him. Then the clerk smartened himself, and a colored bellhop yawned into half-life.

"Mr. Shelton," the clerk said as eagerly as he could manage. "Happy you could come down early."

"No happier than I am," Larry said as he accepted the ballpoint and looked down at the registration card.

"Our hesitancy this morning was prompted by our lack of staff, not overcrowding."

"So I notice."

"Ah, yes. We have a few guests, and of course we'll have a full house and a full complement of employees by Friday."

The woods were lovely. For three days Larry tramped the old familiar trails and explored new ones. The fresh mountain air, cold and sharp in the morning, went deep into his lungs as he climbed through underbrush for fresh vistas of the valleys on either side of the ridge. He carried fruit and sandwiches with him and ate snacks beside newly discovered springs or brisk mountain streams. He told himself that nature was airing out the stench, washing away the poison in which the sordid world of fund raising steeped its captives.

Actually, long before he started back toward the hotel on Friday afternoon, he was eager to sniff the NAFR campfires. He forced himself to climb the knoll he had set as his last day's objective, and consciously slowed his pace to keep from trotting downhill to see who had checked in at Briarcliff during his absence.

In sight of the grounds, he stuck his hands into his pockets and began whistling "I'm an Old Cowhand" as he walked past the row of cars parked in the lot and strolled across the high-columned front porch into the bustling lobby.

Bruce Harvey, of Love Gifts, Ltd., saw him first.

"Larry Shelton," he called. "Boy, do you look like a tramp, the ultimate end of a forgotten money hunter."

"Hi, Bruce," Larry said. "I have been for a tramp in the woods."

"Yeah. I know, like the two old maids." By that time they were shaking hands. "What are you doing here? I heard that you'd been banished from NAFR NAFR Land." Bruce looked like a blond choirboy.

"Is that so?" Larry asked. "I hadn't heard it."

Others were gathering around, effusive in their greetings, openly inquisitive in their glances.

"Don't kid us, boy." Bruce went on. "We've heard the sob story; the little s.o.b.'s, that is. Is that why the Pious One turned you out and made you walk to Briarcliff?"

"Shucks, no." Larry twisted his right hiking boot like a shy plowboy's clodhopper. "I've been here for days. The early bird, you know."

"Yeah, the early vulture."

"Gets the finger," another colleague finished.

"Honest, fellows." Larry stuck to his plowboy. "I've been here three days, having a ball all by myself. I just love the woods this time of year—the autumn colors. The reds, the browns—"

"The long greens," somebody added. "Like you love widows and orphans. What was the widow like, Larry?"

Larry ignored the question.

"I've got to change into uniform," he said instead. "Where's the campfire tonight?"

"In the Diseases teepee. Number three, I think it is— the Hawthorne." All the slaves' quarters were named for trees or shrubs or corruptions thereof.

"That's the big blaze, but there'll be little ones all around," Bruce Harvey said.

"White man buildum big fire, standum way back. Injun buildum little fire, situm up close." The speaker had already been sitting very close to the embers, if the smoke on his breath was honest.

Bruce Harvey accompanied Larry to the elevator and rode up with him.

"You really must have blistered old Chancellor with that cop-survivors caper, Larry," he said.

"Hell, I quit him long before I directed that campaign."

"Well, he's sure sore as hell about something. Our outfit is buzzing. He's trying to queer you with the church crowd. He probably will. With the Schoolboys, too."

"I couldn't care less. Come on in." Larry unlocked his door and stood aside to let his guest precede him.

"He collared the Diseases as they came by the registration desk. Of course, he can't attend their campfire."

"Nope. Firewater is poison to the saints. There's a bottle in the closet. Want some ice?"

"No firewater yet. I have to commune with my saintly Master before dinner." Bruce Harvey plopped onto a chair. "What are you going to do, Larry? You can't live off cops' corpses forever."

"Oh, I have lots of ideas," Larry lied, as he tossed his shirt on the bed. "I can always find a new product. Look at the Diseases. The Dimes people didn't close up shop when they ran out of polio. TB, grandfather of them all, got a new lease on life when emphysema came along."

"Emphysema? Who is she?"

"Grandpa's new mistress. Haven't you been listening?" Larry, stripped, stepped into the bathroom and turned on the shower.

He heard no more until he turned off the spray and came back into the bedroom, toweling his body briskly.

"So you're not here looking for a job?" Harvey asked him.

"Hell, no. I'm a card-carrying member of this brother-hood. I love the fellowship. I might even try for a place on the policy level. By the way, what's on the agenda this year? What are the gripes?" Larry stepped into fresh shorts.

"The government, same as last year. Boy, with Health, Education, and Welfare moving in, the bureaucrats are scaring hell out of everybody. Socialized medicine could take over the Diseases. The prospect of federal aid to education has set the Schoolboys quaking in their sneakers. And Welfare can mean anything from the Milk Fund to the Red Cross.

"Government-controlled philanthropy is Old Man Devil. When IRS turns Santa Claus and makes taxes out of love offerings, NAFR has had it. That's why I'm sticking with God's chillun. As long as we can keep church and state separate, us pickaninnies got bread and meat."

"Sounds bad," Larry said lightly as he tucked in his dress shirt.

"In a way I don't mind seeing the Diseases in pain. They've been the aristocrats so long, the smug fat cats of the trade, that a little misery might do them good. Heart and Cancer and MD and Cerebral Palsy have had it so damned easy, sitting on their fats, with unlimited public-service time on radio and TV, mailmen and local yokels pounding the pavement for them. All they have to do is count it and split it."

"You are maligning my hosts, sir." Larry knotted his tie and reached for his coat.

"I wish I could go with you," Bruce Harvey said, rising, "but it's chillun's hour over in the tabernacle. Not even a cup of sacramental wine."

Larry and his companion went back down to the lobby, in which the crowd had thinned out to a few stragglers at the registration desk, filling out forms and getting their nameplates.

"See you around an Injun fire," Harvey said as he was leaving.

"Sure." Larry went to the registrar for his own tag.

"Hi, Larry," the registrar said, recognizing him.

"Hi. Brand me."

"Larry Shelton," the registrar dictated to the typist pecking on the big-cap machine.

"Firm name?" she asked, when the registrar paused and showed some embarrassment.

"Laurence P. Shelton Associates," Larry said boldly.

She hammered that out and handed the identification tag to the registrar, who ripped the protective tape off its mastic back and stuck the label on Larry's breast pocket.

"Thanks," Larry said, and headed for the Hawthorne.

70

The white man's fire was blazing high, but no one was standing back. Larry pushed his way through the crowded party room of the cottage to the long bar where five white-coated waiters were pouring drinks.

"Scotch and soda. Twist of lemon peel," he said.

The Diseases always served good liquor. As Stanley had said, they were indeed the aristocrats, the fat cats of the trade. The minor ailments who had been forced to pitch in with Community Chests and United Funds and consequently were subject to strict local audits were, of course, no longer considered entities in their own right. But the smart boys with the pathetic pictures and the big fears as ammunition, the ones who could hold their own with Big Government and Big Business and remain accountable to no one—they formed the corporate body of Big Disease. They could afford good liquor.

There was no room for conversation groups in the Hawthorne. Larry caught nods and responded to hails, but actually all he could expect was good whiskey. There was no possibility of feeling the fraternal pulse around this white man's campfire. He would have to wait for the Injun fires. But that was no reason for going out into the cold on a night like this.

11

$ $ $

LARRY ATTENDED THE FIRST GENERAL MEETING AND SAT through an inspiring keynote address by the outgoing president of NAFR, a phenomenally successful hard-sell artist who,

71

in his declining years, had taken a resident job at a denominational college and was still raising over six million dollars a year as a Schoolboy, and who had been elected president as a compromise candidate when neither the Benevolences nor the Diseases could muster a clear majority. The speaker had a lot to say about free enterprise, the American Way, the goodness of man, and a dozen other virtues which might easily be destroyed by a socialistic state bent on robbing its citizens of their basic human happiness—the Joy of Giving.

When committee appointments were announced and the assembly recessed for organizational meetings, Larry found himself with time on his hands. Since as a free agent he fitted into no recognized category, his name was nowhere mentioned on the committee rosters. His position was understandable; yet he did feel strange wandering into the Briarcliff lobby when all the others repaired to the various conference rooms.

It was not that the lobby was empty. Several men were seated on various chairs and sofas—no two together, however, as though they were avoiding one another. Each one looked up, furtively it seemed, as Larry strode through the lobby and sat down in an easy chair before the log fire in the massive fireplace. No one rushed, but almost immediately the nimblest of the guests found a chair next to Larry's.

"You're Larry Shelton, aren't you?" the nimble one asked as he sat down.

"Yes," Larry admitted, almost as guiltily as his neighbor had asked the question.

"Jake Shapiro." He was a small dark man, immaculately turned out and scented by the latest men's spray. "I've heard a lot of good things about you lately."

"And a bad one or two?" Larry asked.

"Depends." Shapiro laughed, softly, confidentially. "I've heard that you're tops in your line—and maybe available. Is that bad?"

"Depends."

"Right. I'd say it was good."

72

"For whom?" Larry asked.

"For you, for me." The little man leaned closer to Larry's chair. "For my brother. He's a doctor, see? We've got a new children's disease."

"Not another one! It's a wonder kids ever grow up." Larry found the latest men's spray offensive.

"But this one makes cerebral palsy and muscular distrophy look like a case of measles. You ought to see our pictures. They'd break your heart."

"They usually do."

"We can plug every angle—mail-outs, stamps, seals, magazines—unlimited radio and TV time. We've got the disease; you have the know-how. We could clean up."

"Not my line," Larry objected.

"Hell, I'm not through yet. We'll build centers and clinics all over the country. Building campaigns, annual sustentation drives. That's where you come in. We know you're good at that. Everybody does."

"Why don't you make your pitch to the Diseases? They're in rooms ten, eleven, and twelve; and I hear they're running scared."

"Yeah. I know. There are already rumors of government-sponsored clinics and research in cancer, heart, and strokes. I intend to contact some of the Disease boys."

"Then why don't you?" Larry was far from cordial.

"I just thought you might be interested."

"I'm not," Larry said.

"O.K., O.K. No harm in trying," Shapiro said peevishly.

"Depends."

The men's spray faded. Again there was no rush, but soon the masculine fragrance of an athlete's deodorant pervaded the fireside area.

This was a guard—or a tackle gone to fat—a big blond bruiser with a trick knee that had to be humored into position before a low chair.

"You Larry Shelton?" the guard asked.

"Yes. What's your pitch? Not another children's disease, I hope." Larry was simmering over the realization that his story was out—outside the trade. He was fair game for chiselers.

"Hell, no. I say keep 'em healthy." The guard came from the Southeastern Conference, or his dialect was phony.

"So do I. What's the gimmick?"

"Boys' Island."

"Boys' Island? Oh, no!" Larry was brutal.

"Why not?" The guard was impervious. He had been needled on the line. "There's a Boys' Town, a Boys' Ranch, a boys' everything else. Why not a Boys' Island?"

"And a Girls' Island?"

"That too." There was some humor in the bland blue eyes. "I've got the island. I can get the boys. The girls are just across the bay, plenty of 'em!"

"Where?"

"Off the coast of Florida—one of the keys. A hotel, with cabañas. A little run-down, losing money. We can take it over. Think of the pitch. The little bastards growing up in the sunshine, swimming, fishing, boating. Hell, it's got it all over towns and ranches."

"Schooling?" Larry asked.

"On the mainland. Run 'em over every morning in a launch."

"The money?"

"Your department. Hell, if you can raise half a million on two little punks, think what you can do with an island of 'em —year in and year out."

So the little s.o.b. take was growing by the usual increments of gossip.

"And we can fix up one suite in that hotel like a palace —live like kings."

"Where'll you get the boys? Off government relief?"

"I mean white kids," the guard said contemptuously.

"To hell with it." Larry rose and headed for the bar. It

74

was eleven o'clock, time for an appetizer or two before lunch.

By the time he got his first drink he had been joined by a military gentleman with a clipped mustache.

"Colonel McBride, general staff," the military identified itself.

"Lieutenant, j.g., Shelton, public information," Larry said brusquely. "Rank doesn't mean a god-damned thing to me."

"So I've heard. Insubordination." The colonel laughed. A drink was set before him.

"Don't tell me that the general staff is out of funds," Larry said.

"Retired," the colonel said affably.

"Me too."

"But hale and hearty, I see. Not all of our comrades-in-arms are so well off."

"So what?" Larry would have got more satisfaction out of snubbing an admiral, but he had to settle for what the moment afforded.

"So I think there are still some veterans' ills that might command public attention and private philanthropy."

"I can't think of any. I'm sure that the military contingent meeting down the hall has scraped the barrel. At least my mailbox seems to fill up with the scrapings about once a month."

"Organizations," the colonel snorted. "The veterans' organizations have worn out their welcome. They can't even be depended on as voting blocs any more."

"Too bad."

"But a little individual effort, a little creative thinking—"

"In the military?" Larry registered shock, and the colonel reddened around his ears.

"Would you like to see a little plan I've worked out?"

"Now, Colonel McBride, you know I haven't had a security check. I couldn't be trusted with top-secret information."

"That's right. You probably couldn't." The colonel drained his glass and swiveled around on his bar stool.

Good for the military. Colonel McBride was the only one who had struck back. Larry was proud of him.

"Hi, Larry," a new voice spoke.

"Hi." Larry turned to see a familiar face at his shoulder. "Jim Bostick! How are you, boy?"

"Fine. Drinking alone?" Jim was a steady, unspectacular United Fund director from the Midwest—balding a little, spreading a little, but complaining not at all.

"Colonel McBride was drinking with me," Larry explained. "He just left. A luncheon, I think. Join me?"

"Sure. Bourbon—straight." Jim eased onto the stool beside Larry. "How about having lunch at my table, now that you're a maverick?"

"Thanks, Jim. That's the best offer I've had so far." Larry nodded to the bartender for another drink.

"You've had others?"

"Sure. A new disease, a veterans' pitch, and Boys' Island."

"Boys' Island." Jim chuckled good-naturedly. "What will they think of next?"

"I have a penthouse for wayward girls in mind."

"You would." Jim made Larry feel a little better, another successful pro talking to him like one of his own kind.

"How's the family?" Larry asked.

"Just fine. I have three boys and a girl now. Two in high school. One in a high chair."

"That's what comes of being home nights."

"Yeah. It's a good life, Larry. Little irritations now and then, of course, but no rat race."

"Are you trying to suck me into UF work—putting all my begs in one asking?" Larry spoke gently, though. He had no quarrel with Jim Bostick.

"Only if you want it. You're a good man. I could get you in somewhere—ten, fifteen, twenty thousand a year."

"How do you boys feel about HEW? It seems to have the others worried."

"Not us, Larry. If the government takes over, we'll still run the show. Who else? We know the business better than anybody."

"I see. Just move over into civil service—bureaucrats, huh?"

"We'd never know the difference; only the tax collectors would carry on our fund drives for us."

"You lazy bastard." Larry laughed. "What would you do for exercise?"

"Play golf in September too." Jim could laugh as easily as Larry. "It ain't bad, boy. It ain't bad."

"But is it fun?"

"My kids are." Jim drained his glass. "Coming to lunch with me?"

"Jim—I—no, I guess not."

"O.K. I see your point. If you joined us here, the hotshots would think that you had thrown in the towel. You've got 'em worried too, Larry. Too worried maybe. The youngsters don't want your kind of competition in their outfits, and the old-timers are afraid you might take over if they hired you. You just might be too big for your breeches."

"Thanks, Jim. You've given me the picture."

"Yeah. I've been listening."

"I appreciate it. I think I'll look for some bigger breeches, though."

"If you don't find any, or if they don't fit, let me know." Jim Bostick left the bar for the UF luncheon table.

The luncheon tickets were good anywhere; so Larry squared his shoulders and went to the Benevolences table, joining the group with which he had last been affiliated. He sat by Bruce Harvey.

"Where have you been all morning?" the choirboy asked.

"Prospecting."

"Any luck?"

"Sure. Four offers in two hours."

Just then David Chancellor began to say grace, which was one of the treats Larry had come for. He listened to the great man's invocation more closely than he ever had before—masochism again. After grace, he chatted with the others around the table—field hands all—but he sensed their hesitancy to appear cordial to him within sight and earshot of their betters. The hypocritical bastards. He was glad that he had been cast out.

He attended two of the afternoon workshops, one before the coffee break and one after. In both he heard more and more about the fear that HEW was going to engulf the country, turn the joy of giving into tax resentment, dry up philanthropy, destroy free enterprise. Later he wandered from cocktail party to cocktail party, hearing more of the same at every Injun fire. Only at the big banquet in the evening, which was more thoroughly covered by the press, did he hear the long-familiar platitudes—the self-congratulations of dedicated humanitarians, the spiritual rewards of being privileged to help direct brotherly love, the national benefits of guidance in giving.

After the banquet came another round of campfires, where the legends of the hunters were retold, the growing saga of NAFR NAFR Land. Larry lingered at one Injun fire long enough to hear an old Benevolence repeat the story of the Rich Old Rancher, the Lovely Young Wife, and the Handsome Top Hand. The payoff had grown through gossip-increments to an entire new church complete with pipe organ. He could remember when the Rich Old Rancher had kicked in with a measly hundred grand.

He heard a mellowing Schoolboy start the one about the Millionaire's Wife's Collection of Butterflies, which an enterprising moocher had parlayed into a four-story library with a museum on top to house the Collection. But he wandered on. He knew all about the costly hand-painted brochure which had turned the trick. Unless the library had expanded over the years, there would be nothing new in that one. He strolled into the middle of a Municipal Fundsman's account of the Doting Grandfather who had been conned into building a whole theatre-center complex for his awkward grand-daughter's debut in *The Dying Swan*.

The Legend of Los Angeles, with its Lady Culture Vulture, was just then being introduced into fund-raising folklore; but, though still fragmentary, it showed promise of developing into a dilly. He listened long at that campfire, which was being fueled by Chivas Regal. From there he moved to a collection of Shame-the-Niggardly-Bastard stories and on to a suite of variations on the Glare-of-the-Public-Spotlight theme. If not glaring, Larry was at least glowing happily, or reflecting the glow of the last dying embers, when he finally tumbled into bed.

He felt comfortably inspired. The hunters' tales, success stories all, restored his confidence. What had succeeded once would succeed again—and again—and again. He had no worries. Who the hell was HEW?

12

SUNDAY MORNING WAS SOMETHING ELSE AGAIN. SUNSHINE on the ridge, a joy in midweek, was a bit harsh on the eyeballs. Larry blinked, tasted the sour inside of his mouth, frowned, pressed his temples, pointed his feet toward the side of the bed, and eased his torso up into a sitting position. Painfully he reached for the telephone and ordered a pot of coffee. Then he made the tortuous journey to the bathroom and suffered the sting of a hard cold shower. He was toweling himself sluggishly when the coffee arrived.

The coffee helped. It made shaving and dressing tolerable, if not enjoyable. No longer one of God's chillun, he was under no compulsion to attend devotionals held in the Benevolences tabernacle. Nor was he drawn to punish himself further by seeking the presence of David Chancellor. He had punishment enough already, throbbing through the loose connections in his nervous system. So he could delay breakfast, perhaps try the hair of the dog, and accustom himself to a reasonably upright position before the final session of NAFR at eleven o'clock.

Larry poured the last cup of coffee out of the pot and picked up the Sunday paper brought in on the tray. It was a Roanoke paper, of no particular interest to him, but he let his eyes scan it just to see if they would work. They did, though nothing of interest passed beyond their retinas. A local contractor was in trouble with the city. A supermarket had been robbed. The foreign-aid program was under attack. The President was plugging his physical-fitness program. *President Plugs Physical Fitness*. The optic nerves began functioning.

The President said that the kids of the country were in horrible shape. They did too much riding, too little walking, too much sitting down, too little pushing up, too much watching, too little participating, etc., etc., etc. Larry subconsciously related that to Boys' Island; only the President was not talking about the all-conference guard's homeless little bastards. He was talking about kids on the mainland, kids everywhere—rich kids, poor kids, privileged kids, underprivileged kids, just kids in general.

Larry forgot that reading was painful. It became easier

and easier and then positively exciting. Those poor, weak, underdeveloped children. They needed youth facilities—Youth Facilities, Youth Directors, Pat Hayden. It would be a shame if any little girl was denied the opportunity to develop into another Pat Hayden. Someone, some dedicated humanitarian with real know-how, ought to do something about the situation before HEW got around to it. Larry reread the story. He so forgot his own physical condition that he dropped the paper on the floor and sprang to his feet.

Springing to his feet was a mistake, a near disaster; but at least he was on his feet and headed toward a new field of philanthropy—headed toward the door, anyway.

He went downstairs and forced himself to order a normal breakfast. Other conventioneers were straggling in and out of the coffee shop. Bruce Harvey stopped at the door and looked around. When he spotted Larry he joined him.

"Matins over?" Larry asked as Bruce sat down facing him.

"Just over. Your erstwhile Master is a long-winded old bastard."

"I know. I can't take his piety on an empty stomach—and I'm having a late breakfast. So—"

"So you skipped devotionals. I envy you. If it wasn't for the present HEW and cry I'd turn apostate myself and join one of the Diseases."

Larry's breakfast came. Bruce gave it a dour appraisal but ordered the same.

"Still think you'll get a place on the policy level?" Bruce asked.

"I wasn't even on the resolutions Committee." Larry tasted his scrambled eggs.

"So I notice, or any other. I'd say you were all washed up if you didn't look a hell of a lot happier right now than a guy ought to look who is as hung-over as you ought to be after last night."

"Watch your rhetoric, Harvey," Larry said. "I can talk better than you're talking, and my mouth's full."

"I guess you've talked yourself into a bright future. Have you?"

"Well, I'm through prospecting."

"What's the new connection? Can I come along? Gad, those devotionals!"

"I said I *could* talk," Larry reminded him. "But I'm not talking."

"I'll be watching you, comrade. So will all the rest of us. If you've found something good, a lot of us may want a piece of it."

"Don't I know it."

Larry did not attend the final NAFR session. Instead he went back to his room, packed, and checked out of Briarcliff before twelve o'clock. He headed for Washington. He could turn the rent car in there as well as in Columbus, though he was momentarily tempted to drive back the way he had come, on the off chance that he might drop in on Pat again. But she probably did not bowl on Sunday evenings; and if his plans worked out, he might have something to offer her soon, something better than a proposal of marriage.

He arrived in Washington late Sunday afternoon. Monday morning he was at the Library of Congress when the doors opened. For the next few days he virtually lived there. He studied yearbooks, government bulletins, municipal reports, and a plethora of similar documents. He memorized files of out-of-town newspapers from every sizable city in the United States. Gradually the full picture began to take shape.

He systematically narrowed his study down to cities in border states, as defined by civil rights advocates, and especially to those that were experiencing postwar booms and becoming aware of their histories of civic neglect. New municipal buildings and civic centers financed by bond issues bespoke ambition, along with a strain on tax revenue for years to come. These conditions plus the nonexistence of a public gymnasium seemed to Larry to define the climate he was seeking.

82

When he collected his notes and made projections from them, everything pointed to Corinth as the lucky city. He checked and rechecked and came up with the same answer. At least it was worth a trip.

Research completed, he telephoned Herb Phillips in New York.

"What's your trouble, Brother-in-Law?" Herb asked. "Need money?"

"Certainly not, this is Larry."

"I know. I know. My rich relative. O.K., what can I do for you?"

"Can you set up a tax-exempt Federal Physical Fitness Foundation, over in Jersey, say?"

"You mean can you call it Federal?"

"Sure. Federal, okay. United States, no.

"Got any capital?"

"I can give away twenty-five or thirty thousand tax-free this year and I might gamble a little more," Larry assured him.

"That ought to do it."

"And I can funnel a million or two more through it in the next twelve months."

"Less fifteen per cent," Herb reminded him.

"Less fifteen per cent to Laurence P. Shelton, Community Funds Consultants. Remember?"

"Yeah. You got some more little s.o.b.'s lined up?"

"Hundreds of them."

"Good. I'm glad you're working again. I hate shiftless relatives."

"Nuts, Counselor. Get on with my legal affairs, and give my love to Katy."

"Will do." Herb hung up.

Larry found the same rent car still in Washington and took two leisurely days to drive to Corinth. He put up at the largest motor hotel in town, so he could remain as anonymous as possible. He ate in crowded restaurants, where his face would not be remembered, and spent two more days cruising around with a Corinth city map open beside him, checking industrial property offered for rent or lease in the newspapers. Warehouses, factory buildings, old lodge halls—he surveyed them all.

At last he found what he was looking for, an abandoned laundry in a run-down neighborhood. The building looked substantial—no firetrap—but it had not been painted in years, and a gang of ragged little boys were in the process of breaking the last windowpanes with a volley of hard coal from the laundry's own bin.

Larry parked across the street from the building and got out of his car. The boys scrambled out of sight in a hurry; but two dirty little girls, nine or ten years old, faced him boldly.

"I'll tell you who done it, Mister," one of them said. Thoroughly scrubbed, she might have been a blonde.

"We ain't broke nothing," the other, a born brunette, assured him.

"I don't care who did it," Larry said. "I don't own the place."

"We know it," said the once-fair one.

"Ain't you a 'tective?" asked the other.

"No. How long has the laundry been closed?"

"A long time," said the blonde. "Mr. Merrit said the wash'terias got him."

"He said laundry-mats," the other corrected her.

"He said wash'terias. I heard him. 'And me with my boilers just barely paid for,' he said to my daddy."

"Where is Mr. Merrit?"

"We don't know. He left."

"He never did live here."

It did not matter to Larry. The building was advertised in the paper, and there was a FOR LEASE sign nailed over the door, with the agent's address and telephone number. He jotted those down and went around peering through various broken windows. The little girls, more curious than he, tagged along and kept up a steady barrage of questions.

The building had been stripped of everything movable, everything except the boilers, which were set in masonry. There were no partitions inside except those near the front, where an office, a receiving counter, and two dressing rooms for employees had been enclosed. It looked just about right for an improvised gymnasium. He thanked his guides for their help and offered them two dimes to buy some candy.

"We can't take candy from strangers," the blonde said.

"We won't get in your car, either," the dark one added.

"O.K. I'll just leave these dimes on the windowsill here and drive off in my car. How will that be?"

"Fine," they said, beaming.

So much for places and things, Larry thought. Now, to people.

He drove nearer to the business section and left his car in a parking lot. He passed along below upstairs hotels, by pawnshops and secondhand stores, through an arcade lined with paperback books and lurid magazines. Three or four panhandlers solicited him.

In my element, he thought, as he turned into a bar which seemed to bridge the gap between the have-littles and the have-nots in Corinth.

"What'll it be?" asked a tubby bartender from halfway down the counter.

"Scotch and soda."

"Bar Scotch?" He noted Larry's clean shirt.

"Peter Dawson." Larry slid onto a bar stool.

"Bar Scotch where I used to work," the barkeep commented. Perhaps Larry's collar had wilted just a little.

"I still like it," Larry said.

" 'Taint bad," the bartender conceded more genially, as he poured the liquor. "Most people don't know it. I don't know why. Old Peter's been with us a long time. Big before prohibition, they tell me."

"I wouldn't know about that."

"Me neither." The barkeep set the drink before Larry.

As Larry's eyes adjusted to the darkened room, it seemed to be empty except for him and his host.

"You worked here long?" Larry asked.

"A year and eight months. I bought the place. Used to work farther uptown, lots of places, a long time."

"You probably know an acquaintance of mine, a newspaperman. He used to be pretty good—hit the skids a few years back." Larry was sure that there was such a person; there was one in every town. "I forget his name. Met him here while I was in the service, had a few drinks with him."

"Thin, kind of sandy-haired, getting bald?"

"That's the one."

"Yeah. Sam Algood."

"That's it. I was about to say Albright. But it *was* Algood. Ever see him around?"

"Sometimes, when he's really in bad shape. Usually he don't get down this far. Got lots of friends uptown—like you, maybe—that'll stand him a drink or two. Hangs out mostly around the Penguin, or did when I worked there."

"I believe that's where I met him," Larry said.

"You a newspaperman?"

"In a way." Larry eased off the bar stool and left a dollar bill under his glass. "Be seeing you."

"Yeah. Hurry back."

Larry walked lazily uptown, peering into bars and show windows, until he came face to face with a man-sized penguin wearing a bow tie. He nodded to the bird and opened the door beside it. This bar had several customers variously engaged at pinball machines, miniature shuffleboards, and domino tables.

"Peter Dawson and soda," Larry said to the bartender, and, when his drink arrived, "Sam Algood been around this afternoon?"

"Yeah. Sure, he was here a minute ago. Anybody seen Sam?" He raised his voice.

"He just went to the crapper," somebody answered.

Larry took his drink over to an empty booth. Presently

he heard the bartender say, "Sam, a guy was just asking about you. In that booth over there."

Sam Algood, easily recognizable from the classic prototype, walked carefully toward Larry's booth. He was thin— emaciated—his clothes touching his body only where they were fastened on, his stubbly face as lean as his frame, and his eyes, when they peered in at Larry, as gray as morning mist, but bloodshot, like the dawn.

"You want me?" he asked.

"I asked about you, yes. Sit down. What are you drinking?"

"Are you kidding? Anything you'll buy."

"I'll buy anything you want."

"I've been drinking rotgut; but I'd like some very Old Fitzgerald, if it's double."

"It's double," Larry said, and summoned a barmaid.

"Remember me?" Larry asked Sam.

"Hell, no. And I remember everybody I ever saw."

"That's understandable—you never saw me before. You used to work on one of the papers—the *Corinthian*, wasn't it?"

"All the papers. *First Corinthian, Second Corinthian,* the *Evening Bladder*—"

"Then you're just the man I'm looking for. I have a proposition to make."

"Like what?" The drink arrived, and Larry noted that Sam was not too far gone to savor his whiskey.

"Like I'll buy you a steak dinner with about a gallon of coffee, and then we'll go somewhere and talk it over."

"What gives, fellow? You don't look like a queer to me."

"Nothing like that. Let's say that I'm a Big Time Operator who needs a writer with real savvy to do a job for me."

"Look, friend, whoever told you about me must have told you I can't hold a regular job." Sam was taking his drink much slower than anyone would have expected. "I'm not drunk enough yet to mislead a stranger."

"Who said anything about a regular job? How about a highly irregular job?"

"Uh-huh. So it's dirty. Sir"—Sam assumed a drunk's outraged dignity—"we Algoods are poor, disreputable, besotted, but we never play dirty." He gulped the second half of his double and prepared to rise.

"Hold it, Sam," Larry said. "It isn't dirty, but it's delicate —and humanitarian. I'll pay what your last regular job paid. You can do most of your work right around these bars, and you won't have to stay sober over two days a week."

"For how long?"

"Six months—a year."

"Starting when?"

"After dinner, if the coffee works. Where can we get a good steak?"

"I know a dump. Commercial cuts cooked by a genius. But you won't be ashamed of me there." Sam was a long way from being drunk. "You'll never know the meat isn't prime, and the coffee's the best in town."

"O.K. Let's go. I have a car parked down the street."

"We can walk," Sam said, and eyed Larry suspiciously.

"You're the third person today who has refused a ride. This is a cautious town."

Sam guided Larry back the way he had come. They turned off on a side street and down into a basement marked by a dingy sign reading *Angelo's*.

Angelo himself showed them to a secluded booth and seated them.

"Two big steaks *à la* Momma," Sam said. "This nice gentleman will pay for them."

"Drinks?"

"I'll drink two cups of coffee as a cocktail," Sam said, meeting Larry's eyes, "because I want a glass of Angelo's wine with my steak. Then I'll drink seven more pints of coffee. I know my capacity."

"You, sir?"

"Coffee, too," Larry said.

"Momma may let the steaks rot first, for all I know," Sam said, after Angelo had gone to the kitchen. "But they come out tasting wonderful, and as tender as your beloved."

The steaks did come out tasting wonderful. And Sam, true to his word, drank one glass of wine and, if not seven pints of coffee, enough to make him appear quite sober.

"All right, stranger, shoot," he said to Larry when the table was cleared. "I don't say I'm buying, but I'll listen. Just what do you have in mind?"

"A gymnasium for the underprivileged and overprivileged kids in Corinth."

"There ain't none."

"That's what I mean. I intend to raise the money to build one."

"What for?"

"For fifteen per cent of the gross."

"That figures. I mean it gives you a motive. Will you really build it? Or will you decamp with the funds you raise? Seems I remember your billing yourself as a BTO."

"I'll build it," Larry assured him. "The funds will go into a chartered foundation that I can't touch. I'll be paid the usual fee by the foundation after the gym is assured. If I don't make it, the money will be returned to the donors."

"Do you know your business?"

"I'm one of the best in that business."

"Surely you don't need me, then. Where do I come in?"

"I know my business. You, presumably, know Corinth and everybody here. I need you to help make the citizens of Corinth aware of the need."

" 'Create the need' is the expression common in the trade, I believe," Sam said with a cadaverous grin. "But I'll buy 'make aware.' There's a need, all right."

"I've determined that."

"And I suppose you've determined how to go about filling it. Are you going to tell me, or do you figure on just buy-

89

ing an old rummy and leading him along by holding a jug just out of his reach?"

"You're my first gamble. If you want to sell the story of a big con game to one of your old newspaper buddies in the morning, you have it now. If you want a sinecure for a year and a part in a humanitarian enterprise, I'll go on. That's the risk I have to take with someone here."

"Go on," Sam said, grinning again. "If I'm going to sell a feature on a con game, I should have enough details to make it sound convincing."

"Within the next few weeks the Federal Physical Fitness Foundation will rent a suitable building for a temporary gymnasium. A team of athletic directors will be sent in to implement the health program. They'll renovate the building, enroll a bunch of sickly, half-starved kids, and feed and exercise those kids for a year."

"And there should be pictures of the kids before and after," Sam cut in, "and a little story now and then about the dedicated work of the athletic directors."

"You get the idea. After a few months there should be letters to the editors from interested persons."

"Coached by me in certain carefully chosen bars and taverns."

"Perhaps even dictated." It was Larry's turn to grin.

"Until a ground swell demands full community participation."

"Who's writing this script?" Larry asked.

"You called me a writer once."

"You *were* a writer once," Larry said soberly.

"That I was. That I was."

"And you must still have connections. I said the job was delicate, but it isn't dirty and it isn't crooked."

"And not too irregular," Sam said. "I've been conned by cruder operators in my time. How much do you think the gym will cost?"

"I had a million dollars in mind."

"And fifteen percent of that is a hundred and fifty thousand."

"Less your stipend," Larry reminded him, "and a great many incidental expenses—like the cost of a good man to find out for sure who can give how much. You'll help there.

"And you'll give me a line on the little people I'll need to carry on the campaign—not too bright scoutmasters, busybody spinsters, frustrated matrons, and so on—people who can be led until I am called in to do the fund raising. Then I'll get the big people lined up, the ones who really matter. But until I am definitely employed it'll be up to you and the staff of the temporary gym."

"If I can be depended on," Sam said, "to stay sober two days a week."

"If you can be depended on," Larry agreed. "And if you'll buy it."

"You really intend to build a gym?"

"Yes. You can check on me."

Sam took several long drags on his cigarette.

"I'll buy it," he said at last.

"O.K. You're hired. How much did your last regular job pay?"

"A lousy hundred bucks a week. I've made a lot more in my time. But my last job—"

"A lousy hundred bucks a week it is. I'll pay you a week in advance right now."

Larry counted five twenties out of his wallet and handed them to Sam.

"That will buy a lot of rum," he said.

"It'll buy enough," Sam said, and grinned, more like a cadaver than ever.

13

$ $ $

"HOW WAS CORINTH?" KATY ASKED WHEN LARRY ENTERED THE apartment on his return home."

"Seems ideal."

"So much for the place. What about people?"

"I've hired one, on a gamble. He may work out. He may not. And I have a list of others that I intend to interview. But they'll be employed by the foundation. How is Herb doing with the organization?"

"The papers are all in order, I believe. He left them on your desk for you to look over."

"Larry thanked her and went on into his own room. He sat down at his desk immediately, to examine the documents even before he unpacked his bags. In fact, he was pretty sure that Katy would unpack for him if he stalled long enough.

Herb had done a good job on the Federal Physical Fitness Foundation of New Jersey. Herb, Katy, two other members of Herb's law firm, and a well-known but reasonably respectable politician from Jersey made up the board of directors. Herb had set himself up as chairman and Katy as secretary and treasurer. Larry had put thirty thousand into the original endowment. A Newark bank was named trustee.

He went to work on staff. He chose three names from a

list he had made during his research at the library: a junior-high coach who had been released without stated cause by the school board in a suburb of Cleveland, a basketball star who had been dropped from a Maryland college for shaving points during an NCAA tournament, and a promising Golden Gloves champion who had turned pro and run out of promise. Mavericks all—but competent athletes blackballed by their hypocritical fraternity, boys who just might be grateful enough for the chance at a good job to prove loyal, for a year at least.

He spent the afternoon locating his prospects by devious telephone calls, and then sent telegrams to all three setting up interviews and promising to wire travel money if they answered.

That night he briefed Herb on the entire setup and had him start negotiations for the lease of the laundry by the Federal Physical Fitness Foundation. He also had Katy write to Pat Hayden on Herb's stationery.

"How does this girl fit in with your other outlaws?" Katy asked. "Is she a loose woman or something special?"

"Something special."

"The kind of girl you'd bring home to meet Mother? Or Sister, in this case?"

"The very same."

"Did you find her in the library? I notice that you have no dossier on her."

"Not exactly," Larry said. "She worked on the Calvary Church campaign with me."

"From which you came directly to quit Christian Benevolences, Inc. I smell a rat—or Chanel Number Five. It couldn't be chypre, could it?"

"On Pat Hayden? Not a chance," Larry said with a laugh.

"It says 'Patricia' here. You say 'Pat.' The fragrance lingers on." Katy owled her eyes wisely and went to Larry's typewriter to address the envelope. "Air mail, no doubt," she said.

"No doubt."

The Golden Gloves champion was never heard from. One look at the ex-coach from the Cleveland suburb convinced Larry that he was not to be trusted with little boys. But Slim MacGregor, a clean-cut six-feet-four of wiry muscle, looked good from the beginning. He was intelligent, too. His keen blue eyes guarded Larry's every movement of face or body during the pious pitch about the aims of the Federal Physical Fitness Foundation.

"Sure, I like kids, and I can do just exactly what you want done in your physical-fitness program," he assured Larry, although he spoke warily. "And I'm all for the President and his ideas on health. But something bugs me."

"What?" Larry asked. They were talking in a client's room at Herb's office.

"Why did you latch onto me? The only thing I'm known for is getting into trouble with the NCAA, and I don't think that's the best recommendation a guy can offer."

"The whole thing is a rehabilitation program—for the kids as well as for the people who work with them. Maybe you deserve a second chance. How does that sound?"

"It *sounds* all right, but it don't smell so good. Maybe you're looking for a dumb athlete to front some sort of racket. That's what I am—a dumb athlete, but I know all about these health clubs and things like that. I'm not too dumb, not as dumb as I was a couple of years ago."

"I don't think you're dumb at all, Slim. The foundation is legitimate. Its funds are secure, its program sound. You'll start from scratch, and you'll have to work hard, but you'll get five thousand a year and you'll be rendering honorable service in a humanitarian venture. What's wrong with that?"

"That's what I'm trying to find out." Slim's eyes were keener than ever. Larry would have hated to try to fake a basketball around him. "Look, Mr. Shelton," he blurted out suddenly, "I made one mistake, but I'm not about to make another. I've watched dirty players; I've talked to gamblers;

94

I've been approached by crooked coaches. Now, I'm talking to you. No offense, but you've got an angle."

Larry laughed, not very heartily. He would certainly rather have Slim on his team than on the opponents'.

"Suppose you just turn your nickel over and let me see the other side," Slim went on in earnest. "If it's tails I'll play ball, but if they're both heads I'll clam up and go back to my job at the loading dock. I won't expose your racket."

"You *have* been talking to gamblers," Larry observed.

"Just once."

"Twice. I think I'm going to gamble on you, Slim."

Larry proceeded to outline his plan to Slim, just as he had outlined it to Sam Algood. After all, his own workers had to know the score, if only to avoid stupid slip-ups along the line. And Slim reacted in very much the same way that Sam had reacted.

"Are you really going to build that gym, Mr. Shelton?" he asked when Larry had finished.

"Yes. I'll build it, or the foundation will return all donations. I can't gyp anybody."

"Have you ever built a gym?"

"No, but I've raised the money for lots of churches. I can give you a list of them."

"Why aren't you still building churches?" Slim asked— a reasonable question.

"I'd rather build gyms."

Slim pondered Larry's answer for several seconds. His gaze wandered around the room, his eyes no longer watchful —thoughtful rather, clouded over.

"I think I see your point, Mr. Shelton," he said at last. "If I were you, I think I'd rather build gyms than churches. But you really will build that gym in Corinth?"

"I intend to, and I've never come up short on a campaign yet."

"O.K., Coach, send me in," Slim said, with unclouded eyes and a big smile.

"Mr. Phillips will draw up your contract with the foundation," Larry said, rising. "You really aren't working for me, you know."

"Want to bet?" Slim asked, still smiling.

"My bet's already down."

Pat Hayden still to go, Larry thought, as he left Herb's office. In fact, he thought about Pat Hayden off and on all day, until the time she showed up at Herb's office for her interview. She looked as radiant as ever.

"Larry!" she exclaimed in surprise when she was shown into the client's room, not knowing who was to interview her. No other emotion was apparent.

"Hi, Pat." Larry took her hand, firm and honest.

"I hadn't expected to see you," she said.

"No. My approach was somewhat devious, I'll admit. I was afraid that you might not come if I wrote you myself. After all, you refused to marry me."

"And why not? If the letter means what it says." She made him feel like a heel, looking for suspicion in a mind that knew none.

"Oh, it does. Indeed it does," Larry said, relieved. "Sit down."

He moved around and sat down so that the desk was between them. As she straightened her skirt, he considered how difficult it might be to keep a desk between them if they worked in the same office day after day. It was just as well that she was being interviewed for a job in the field, at first.

"How have you been?" he asked.

"Fine. A little despondent at times, perhaps. I am still somewhat hesitant about applying for a job. I'd have to give references, and well, you know, we talked about that."

"You need no references here," Larry assured her. "Not with me." If he was aware of *double entendre* in his words, it was lost on Pat.

"Will I be working with you, for you?"

"Yes and no. It's a little complicated." In the face of Pat's unwavering honesty and directness Larry had no choice but to plunge immediately into an explanation of his scheme. He omitted nothing, softened nothing.

"So, you see," he said in conclusion, "I'm interested in fund raising—on the same basis that I directed the Calvary Church campaign. I've told you that fund raising can be messy, and you've seen for yourself." He had put himself on the defensive.

"But Calvary Church is being built." Her face went wistful for a moment. "It might never have been built without your help."

"Thanks," Larry said shortly.

"And you really will build a gymnasium in Corinth?" There was that question again. It kept cropping up. Everyone he talked to asked it. Everyone—everyone but Larry—had an eye on the gym.

"Yes," Larry answered, and then doggedly went on. "I'll build the gymnasium, Pat. The difference is that Calvary Church invited me to help. In Corinth, I am going to create" —he brutally adopted Sam Algood's phrase—"the demand, and then come in and raise funds to meet it. And I'm asking you to help. That's the messy part." He stared at her defiantly.

"Doesn't Corinth have a public gymnasium?" Pat asked.

"No."

"Then a city that size certainly should have one." Pat was positive in her statement.

"But who am I to tell them they need one?"

"Who else? Somebody should," Pat pointed out matter-of-factly. "The government does it all the time—tells people what they need, and then supplies it."

And keeps a hell of a lot more than fifteen per cent in service charges, too, Larry thought; but if Pat Hayden considered the practice moral, then, by God, it was moral.

"So you'll go along with us?" he asked.

"Of course. It'll be wonderful to start working with kids

again." What Pat needed was a home of her own, with a house full of kids—her own.

The thought was frightening, so frightening that it smothered a hardy young idea growing in Larry's mind—the idea of taking Pat out on the town for the evening to see what luck he might have with her on his home ground. So, in spite of the new eagerness in her face, the hint of gratitude in her manner, and the magnetism of her handshake, he turned her over to Herb for contractual business and offered simply to accompany her back to the airport, an offer she refused as graciously as she had rejected his proposal of marriage.

Well, Corinth was coming up, and a new campaign.

14

$ $ $

AS SOON AS HERB SECURED A LEASE ON THE OLD LAUNDRY BUILD-ing, Larry called Pat and Slim back to New York for a final briefing. Katy invited them to the apartment for a buffet dinner.

Young MacGregor arrived first, in a dark-gray Ivy League suit. Introductions over, Larry said, "I've been think-ing. *Slim* won't do for your name in Corinth. What's your given name?"

"Angus."

"*Scotty* it is," Larry said, "unless you object."

98

"O.K. with me. Dad was *Scotty* to everybody at home."

"What'll you have to drink, Scotty?" Katy asked. "Whisky? Martini?"

"I'll just watch, if you don't mind," he said easily.

"Oh, yes—I forgot that we were a part of the health program," Katy said. "You're O.K., Scotty. Sit down and I'll look after the mental health of my own two patients. It's past their therapy hour already."

Pat Hayden arrived before Katy could mix drinks for Herb and Larry.

"My big brother can sure pick 'em," Katy exclaimed, as admiring of Pat's healthy young beauty as were the men. "Do you want a drink, Pat? Or do you want to watch, with Scotty?"

"I'll watch, thank you."

After Katy served drinks, she sat sipping a martini for a few minutes before unobtrusively returning to the kitchen. The young couple appeared to be at ease, and as the conversation continued Larry became more and more pleased with Laurence P. Shelton's Associates, once removed. They could hardly miss in Corinth.

The dinner went as easily as the cocktail party had gone, but with hearty participation by the athletic department. The talk was about everything but the business in hand, which Larry kept out of the conversation until Herb had spread the contents of his brief case out on the cocktail table back in the living room.

"Here are all the papers you will need to take over the building in Corinth," Herb said by way of introduction. "The lease, blueprints of the old laundry, your license to operate the place—all in the name of the Federal Physical Fitness Foundation. You will, of course, have to take out health cards after you get there."

"A cinch," Katy observed. "If I ever saw a healthy pair!"

Herb, sitting between the two youth workers on the divan, went over each document, with them looking on raptly.

"And last," he said, "here is a letter of credit from the Newark bank, the trustee, naming either or both of you as agents. Katy, of course, will have to sign all checks on the foundation, but we'll see that you get whatever you need as quickly as possible."

Larry was glad to see Scotty take over the blueprint and start scanning the floor plans.

"How does it look, Scotty?" he asked.

"Pretty good. Of course I'll have to see the building itself."

"You're in for a shock. It looks like a wreck."

"We'll fix it up," Pat said eagerly.

"Not so fast," Larry warned. "Of course you'll fix it up. But I want a picture of you when you first see it."

"A picture? Oh, I get it—"

"I doubt that you do. I mean a real picture, a picture of you and Scotty surveying the *Hesperus*, grim but brave in the face of disappointment, surrounded by a bunch of the dirtiest, raggedest, skinniest little kids you can collect. They're there—I've seen them. In fact, I have a couple of girl friends in the neighborhood.

"And I want that picture on the front page—or some page —of the local newspapers. *The Corinthian*—'the *First Corinthian*, the *Second Corinthian*, and the *Evening Bladder*,' to quote another associate of mine."

Larry chuckled at the memory of Sam Algood, and then frowned as he wondered just how much of the four hundred dollars he had paid Sam so far had gone for rotgut.

"Then you can begin fixing the place up," he continued. "It has to be glazed first. I saw the last windowpanes go myself. I want pictures of you two, smeared with putty, installing glass in the first window. You can hire the rest done after the photographers leave.

"Next the Corinthians will be treated to a view of the indomitable humanitarians on stepladders, painting the front of the building."

100

"A little cheesecake would go nicely there, Pat," Katy suggested.

"For mental health," Herb added.

"But all those photographers," Pat said, frowning. "Will they be there?"

"On cue," Larry said. "And that brings us to Sam Algood. He's a first-rate newspaperman, now numbered among the President's beloved unemployed. Ostensibly. Actually he's on my payroll. I trust him to see that such of your activities as we want publicized are publicized, but good. I'll give you his address and phone number.

"But back to the painting. You can hire it done, too; but spread it out over several weeks, even months. Get some painters to work after hours."

"The smell of paint will make the kids sick," Pat said practically.

"Bright girl," Herb said. "That's what we hired you for."

"O.K.," Larry said. "Leave the inside unpainted, or figure out a schedule yourself, Pat. It was your objection."

"I will," Pat said. He was sure she would.

"Heat will be no problem," Larry said. "There are good boilers in the building. You could even heat water for a swimming pool—one of those plastic jobs."

"Oh, could we?" Pat asked eagerly.

"A small one," Larry said. Her enthusiasm should make it Olympic size for the kids. "A used one, in fact, if you can find one—and there should be some for sale, now that summer swimmers have been faced with the problem of storing the silly things. You might even have one donated. Ask Sam."

"About other equipment," Scotty interrupted.

"The same. Get what you need, but stick to bare necessities. Buy used stuff. Have yourself photographed renovating it and painting it. If you get everything you want, you won't seem to need community support. You have to be seen poorboying it. Two dedicated youngsters struggling against almost

101

impossible odds to carry out the President's physical-fitness mandate."

"We can't expect Larry to give us everything, Scotty," Pat said. "We have to do something ourselves."

Larry looked at her in amazement. He never ceased to wonder.

"I haven't said a dozen words," Scotty muttered defensively.

"And they didn't constitute an objection," Katy said.

Scotty smiled his gratitude.

"How many kids will the place accommodate?" Pat asked.

"More than your budget will allow," Larry said. "You've got to fatten up some of them. You can have more in, but the ones for the before-and-after pictures must be hand picked and nurtured with loving care."

"How many?" Pat repeated.

"Herb has given you your budget figures. You'll have to have milk. Maybe you can mooch some of it from the Milk Fund. And one hot meal a day. You can hire some woman in the neighborhood to cook part time."

"I can cook," Pat said.

"O.K. As you wish, but take care of the nucleus."

"He means groom the show animals, Pat," Katy said with more bite than her gibes usually carried.

Larry gave some further briefing, including how to get in touch with Sam Algood. When he asked for questions at the end, he felt like a drill sergeant, a stupid career soldier instructing bright new recruits who already knew more about the job at hand than he would ever know.

"Can't you come along and help us get started?" Scotty asked.

"Not me. I can't show my face in that town until I'm officially called in as a fund raiser." At last Larry was privileged to make The Appearance.

"And that reminds me," Scotty persisted. "Who's supposed to have invited *us?* Can we just go in and set up shop on our own?"

"Sure. Who invited Jane Addams to Chicago? Albert Schweitzer to Africa? The civil rights workers to Alabama? *Nobody.* Nobody invites do-gooders anywhere—they just move in. You and Pat are do-gooders. I'm a fund raiser. There's a difference."

"I guess so, if you say so."

"We'll make out, Scotty," Pat assured him

With that the staff of the Corinth Laundry Gymnasium rose and prepared to leave.

Katy closed the door behind them.

"Bastard, bastard, bastard," she said to Larry. "Conning those beautiful, wonderful babies into digging your gold mine for you."

"They'll get along," Herb said in frank approval.

"Together," Katy added. "Maybe better than Larry would like. Eh, Big Brother? Never before this minute have I questioned our sainted mother's fidelity. But you—you— Anyway, I've seen you in action."

She pecked Larry on the cheek and went to clear off the table.

"They'll do all right," Herb repeated.

"I hope," Larry agreed. "But I may end up simply promoting the President's health program instead of raising funds."

"You mean your associates can't keep their minds on the real goal of this operation?" Katy asked from the dining room. "I keep forgetting the virtues of the gadfly myself."

"We'll see when the reports start coming in," Larry said.

The first report came in three days later, about nine o'clock in the evening. It was a collect telephone call from Pat.

"Something terrible is wrong here," she said anxiously.

"What?"

"Well, it's about your friend Sam Algood."

"Go on."

"Well, we called his boardinghouse yesterday and again today. His landlady said he was ill."

"Yes?"

"Well, we went to see him. He isn't sick, Larry. He's drunk, dead drunk."

"You don't say." He had to grin at the shock Sam must have given Pat, serious though the situation might be.

"Yes. Disgusting. Why you ever expected him to be of any help."

"Where are you now?"

"In a phone booth about two blocks from his boarding-house."

"Where's Scotty?"

"Outside, guarding the phone booth. It's dark down here."

"O.K. Can you put him on?"

"You want me to?"

"Yes, do."

"Hello, Mr. Shelton," Scotty said a few seconds later.

"Hello. Listen, Scotty. Have you ever had any experience with drunks?"

"Some—a little."

"Fine. Call a taxi. Send Pat home. Then you go back to Sam's room. Get him up—you're a lot bigger than he is.

"Dress him, if he's undressed. Call another taxi and take him to one of those health clubs you detest so. They'll know what to do. They're used to drunks."

"Yes, sir."

"Stay with him. Have him steamed, boiled, massaged—whatever they do—but stay with him. Got it?"

"Yes, sir."

"When they say he's ready, feed him whatever they suggest. Have him cleaned up, shaved, dressed. Buy some clean clothes if he needs them."

"Yes, sir."

104

"When he's rational and presentable call Pat, and both of you take him to dinner at Angelo's."

"Angelo's?" Scotty asked.

"Yes. Sam knows where it is."

"O.K. I've got it."

"Sure you have, Scotty. And let me know how you come out."

"Yes, sir."

"Tell Pat goodbye for me."

Larry heard the click of the receiver hanging up. He cradled his own telephone and sat looking at it for several minutes. Ordinarily two good bets out of three was a fair payoff, but in his gamble it had to be three out of three in the beginning. Without Sam, Pat and Scotty might do a wonderful job feeding the kids and building their bodies; and the Federal Physical Fitness Foundation of New Jersey—meaning Larry Shelton—might very well turn out to be an unintentional philanthropist to the tune of thirty or forty thousand dollars.

So Larry sweated out Sam's de-intoxication—he might as well have been in the same steam chamber—hour after hour. All night, all the next day, another night, four more days, midnight. Pat called again, collect.

"Larry?" she asked when he said, "Hello."

"Yes."

"Scotty said you wanted to know how we came out— with Sam, I mean."

"We?" Larry asked.

"We? Oh, of course, *we*. We're teammates, aren't we? You don't think I'd let Scotty wear himself out, do you?"

"No, on second thought, I guess not." Larry always had to second-think Patricia Hayden.

"Well, we went back to Sam. We bathed him and dressed him, like you said."

Larry did not remember saying anything about bathing Sam.

105

"Then we called a taxi, like you said, and took him to a sanatorium."

"I said health club."

"They wouldn't let me in at the health club."

"That figures," Larry observed.

"The taxi driver said he knew a place, and took us to it. And we stayed with him—on shifts, one of us always—until he was well again."

"*Sober* is the word. You yourself said he was drunk, not sick," Larry reminded her.

"Yes, I did. Well, we got him some new clothes, clean shirts—clean everything."

"Bill me."

"And when he was well enough we went to Angelo's, like you said. Aren't Momma's steaks wonderful?"

"Wonderful. As tender as your beloved."

"That's what Sam said."

"I know."

"And inexpensive. Scotty and I ate two apiece. And we let Sam drink one glass of wine. Momma and Angelo said it was all right. Was it?"

"They know Sam better than we do. Was it all right?"

"I think so. Anyway Sam didn't show any signs. Isn't he brilliant?"

"Yes, isn't he."

"And witty and wise."

"Yes, isn't he," Larry said again.

"He had already set up the stunt, he said, with extras, before we got here."

"So?"

"So tomorrow you can have your picture of me and Scotty getting our first glimpse of the *Hesperus*."

"I look forward to seeing it. You think Sam will do, then."

"Oh, yes, isn't he wonderful?"

"Yes, isn't he." As long as he managed to stay sober two days a week. The thought set Larry to pacing the floor. Never

106

before had he had to stay in the Home Office and trust a campaign to subordinates, and an untried crew at that: two young dreamers and an unregenerate rummy.

And this was only the first week. He wondered if he could stand the strain. His only satisfaction lay in the assumption that David Chancellor must have experienced the same uneasiness a thousand times over.

15

$ $ $

MONDAY MORNING LARRY RECEIVED HIS FIRST TEARSHEETS, VIA air mail, from Sam Algood. The *Corinthian* and the *Evening Journal* both had carried stories and pictures in their Sunday issues. The stories were discreet, scarcely more than notices that the Federal Physical Fitness Foundation had leased the premises of the defunct Merrit Laundry and had sent two of their own health directors to staff a settlement house/gymnasium in the old building.

The pictures, though briefly captioned, said a great deal more. Whoever had posed them had done an artful job. Pat and Scotty stared half-happily at their establishment while a handful of scrawny youngsters stared at them.

"Pipe that luggage!" Katy said, peering over Larry's shoulder. "You'd think Pat and Scotty had come directly from the train—and they've been there a week."

"Empty bags, no doubt, but effective," Larry commented. "So eager to get on with their work that they stopped by to inspect the building before even looking for a place to live. If Sam thought one up, he's exceeding expectations."

"One more picture like this, and the Peace Corps will be drafting your pigeons, Big Brother."

"I'll bet Shriver has none better."

"And his cost him ten thousand dollars per copy, or so the papers say."

"It must be my charm," Larry said.

"Charm, hell. It was blackmail, plus the old come-on. I seen you when you done it."

"Please remember they're working for you and Herb, not for me."

"Come to think of it, we're all working for you. Bastard, bastard, bastard." But there was admiration in Katy's voice.

Larry felt lost, with nothing to do but wait. Given more working capital, he could have been prepping three or four campaigns at once. Too bad he did not have David Chancellor's human resources, dozens of church congregations working for him gratis.

He went back to the Library and continued to add likely prospects—people, places, and things—to his files. Nevertheless, he was restless. He had never fished. How could a man enjoy dropping a hook into the water and just waiting, waiting, waiting for a fish to take the lure? Hunting was his game. Stalk your quarry and gun it down. As it stood, he was powerless even to haul up his line and look at the bait.

Another picture came a few days later—Pat and Scotty glazing one of the front windows, to the wonderment of the same gang of little vandals who had broken the former panes. Then, a week or so later, Pat and Scotty dutifully perched on stepladders, painting the façade, under a professional sign:

CORINTH BRANCH
FEDERAL PHYSICAL FITNESS FOUNDATION

"I guess it *is* too cold in Corinth for pure, unadulterated cheesecake, as I suggested," Katy remarked, kibitzing as usual. "But Pat is certainly doing all any gal could do for that sweater and those ski pants."

"Fetching," Larry agreed.

"Fetch and carry. That girl is carrying out every one of your suggestions to the letter. Is she always so obliging? Has she done everything you've ever—O.K., O.K.—off limits.

"I promised not to probe into the Calvary Church affair, but I claim freedom of thought, freedom of opinion, and freedom of conscience—which I doubt that you're enjoying at the moment."

"I'm reading," Larry reminded her.

The Corinth staff corresponded only with Katy, as secretary of the foundation, and kept all their letters formal and businesslike, inspection-proof by any standard. Sam, on the other hand, was an Associate of Laurence P. Shelton, free to write as he pleased—only, he did not please. He simply mailed tearsheets. One, with a picture of Thanksgiving dinner on a temporary table set up in the bare but tidy old building, bore marginalia in a feminine script, *Turkey and all the fixings, courtesy of the Corinth Press Club, prepared by Momma.* Larry recognized the feminine hand as Pat's, the fine Italian one as Sam's.

Pictures of the Christmas party were more festive, with a tree befitting the spacious hall—massive enough to render pitiably small the peaked faces of the little guests.

"They break your heart," Katy observed, with real tears in her eyes.

"That's the idea," Larry said.

"God damn you, Big Brother, I hope you do some good in that town."

"He'll do them good," Herb said, but Katy looked up at him too late to see which way he meant it.

There were no more stories or pictures for a while, during the post-New Year's lull. In a report to the foundation,

Pat noted the gift of a plastic swimming pool to be added to the inventory, which already included basketball goals, tumbling mats, parallel bars, large and small gym horses, and a number of other odds and ends of equipment she and Scotty had collected.

Her activities schedule included a morning nursery for the very young while their mothers were doing domestic chores, two calisthenics sections for preschoolers in the early afternoon, followed by a three-o'clock period and a four-o'clock period for elementary- and junior-high-school students. She had indeed augmented her milk allowance by a quota from the local Milk Fund and had worked miracles, according to Katy, in spreading her hot-meal budget to feed twenty of the neediest cases.

Soon after Easter a tearsheet arrived with a story headed *Early Spring in the Laundry*. Accompanying the article was a picture of the heated swimming pool full of paddling mites. Scotty, holding a kind of shepherd's crook for quick-rescue purposes, stood beside Pat, who was suited out as instructor and superb example of what clean living and wholesome exercise could do for the human body.

"Now we are bringing our goals out into the open," Katy observed. "Publicizing, but good."

"But good," Larry agreed.

"Just how far along are we really?" she asked.

"About halfway. Corinth holds its United Fund drive in September. I'd like to give the people about a month to forget its bite and then move in—say next November."

"You're getting close to Christmas."

"For this job I believe the time would be right. Since we're concentrating on the have-nots, the haves should feel guiltier during their very early Christmas shopping than at any other time of the year."

So the weeks rolled on into months. The work of the Federal Physical Fitness Foundation was in the news just enough to keep the Corinthians aware of its presence in their city.

Toward the end of school, Larry finally got a letter from Sam Algood:

Dear Big Time Operator [it began]:

It's baseball time in the boondocks. Nothing, except the weather, is quite so hot as Little League in Corinth during the summer months.

I've broached the subject to Pat and Scotty, who now refer me to you. They say they'll be swamped at the gym and, although Scotty has been working with a 10-to-12-year-old team after gym hours for several weeks now, he won't be able to spare the time to make serious contenders out of his club when the season gets into full swing.

Now, it just happens that a first-rate drinking partner of mine, an old pro many years out of the big leagues (as well as out of funds) but plenty long on savvy, has time on his hands—twenty-four hours a day, to be exact. If you think you could spare, say another thirty or forty bucks a week in rum money—I wouldn't want to put him onto a better thing than I have myself, professional pride—he just might be able to make champions out of your charges over across the tracks. Another lousy five hundred bucks should turn the trick, and it could pay off handsomely in good will and hard cash, come the campaign.

You can mete the money out weekly so you won't lose the entire nut if the coach doesn't pan out. I can raise the uniforms and gear among local sportswriters. Let me know how the proposition listens.

Yours for the health of the nation,
J. Samuel Algood

So Larry's only full-time Associate had gone into the fund-raising business himself. For whose specific benefit? For whose rum? Larry wondered. Perhaps it was time for a conference with his sole Associate. He thought the matter over and put in a call to Sam, who, the landlady said, was out, and whose time of return was highly unpredictable. Larry instructed her to leave a note for Sam, and sat around all afternoon waiting for an answer.

It was nine o'clock before Sam returned the call.

"Home kind of early, aren't you?" Larry asked.

"Had a hard day. You got my letter, I suppose."

"Right. I'd like to talk it over with you. Can you come to New York? At my expense, of course. I don't want to show my face in Corinth yet."

"Sure. I work for you."

"Or would you rather I met you somewhere closer home?" Larry was having misgivings.

"No, I like to travel," Sam said.

"You can fly up, if you prefer. I mean if you'd rather not spend time on a train."

"What's the matter? Do you think I'm an alcoholic or something?" Sam chuckled at the other end of the line.

"Choose your poison."

Sam flew. He came to the apartment, since he had no connection with the foundation and Larry still had no office. Sam was neatly dressed. His color was good, and he had put on a few pounds.

Katy offered him a drink, somewhat cautiously.

"I'll just watch, thank you. I'm driving."

"You've seen Scotty in action," Katy said.

"I've seen Scotty in all kinds of action. That boy is good. Either he's the least lazy athlete I ever saw, or Pat needles him like a hornet."

"How is Pat?" Katy asked.

"She's Pat—and in my book that's tops. They're both dynamos. If your brother doesn't raise the money for their gym, they'll skin him alive. The weird thing is that they think you're a grand guy, Shelton."

"That's only half weird," Larry said. "Pat thinks *you*

112

are wonderful—brilliant, witty, and wise, I believe she added."

"Perceptive girl. Bears out my high opinion of her," Sam said smugly.

"Who's your coach?" Larry asked, getting around to the purpose of Sam's visit.

"Red Holloway. Remember him?"

"Red Holloway? Let me see—"

"Infielder—utility man. Played in both the majors. He had some family trouble, dropped to the minors—the farms. Then to the semi-pro and sandlot. Sandlot doesn't pay, you know. Anyway, he's available."

"Could you—could anyone steady him?"

"I don't know, but it's worth a try."

"Has he ever worked with boys?"

"Not that I know of, but he's worked with baseballs all his life."

Larry studied Sam for a minute or two. Just how many more misfits could he depend on? How long would his luck hold out?

"O.K.," he said at last. "Put Holloway on the payroll."

"Good. I'm almost positive he'll make it."

"Now, one more chore for you. What do you know about Mid-Central Market Surveys? I found the firm listed in Corinth."

"They do all right locally, it seems."

"Know any of the personnel?"

"A statistician—used to be with the *Corinthian*," Sam said.

"I need someone to give me a rundown on your charities —their donor lists if available, organizers, volunteer workers —in short, a preliminary survey of the philanthropy potential in Corinth."

"Mid-Central could do that, I'm sure. They know all about Corinth."

"I also need the names of some inept do-gooders in town, the ones who go all out for weak causes and never accomplish anything. You'll have to find those for me—brief mention in back files of the newspapers."

Sam nodded. "I can find them—I know the ones you mean."

"We'll start with them, give them their first chance to launch a really successful venture. I want them organized into the original steering committee, the one that calls me in. Can you manage that?"

"I think so."

"Pat can help, and possibly Scotty can too. Pat has worked with me on a campaign before. Certainly I want them in a position to name the fund-raising agency."

"Otherwise—" Sam chuckled.

"Otherwise I've been had. So, see to it that nobody with ideas of his own gets in on this deal before I have a signed contract."

"I know of some pretty stupid old biddies, of both sexes, and some other types who will fill the bill. I'll see what I can do."

"Fine," Larry said. "Now, are you sure you don't want a drink?"

"I'm sure I won't *take* a drink," Sam said, rising. "I'll just trundle on back out to the airport and fly home. Thanks for taking Red Holloway on. I hope you won't be disappointed in him."

The next Larry heard from Sam was a short clipping announcing the acceptance of a new club into Little League— the Federals—to be sponsored by the Federal Physical Fitness Foundation, managed by Sam Algood, and coached by C. W. (Red) Holloway. *Managed by Sam Algood*. Larry read the announcement again—in dismay. A pack of little nobodies managed and coached by a pair of alcoholics—that was just what he needed to sink the *Hesperus* for good.

He grabbed the telephone at once, to call Sam and cancel him out; but he hesitated. There was the announcement, down in black and white, for all of Corinth, including Pat and Scotty, to see. He cradled the receiver and used both hands to squeeze his temples. Of course somebody had to goof somewhere along the line, but did it have to be the BTO himself?

Larry released his temples with a groan. He turned to his typewriter and sent in subscriptions to the *Corinthian* and the *Evening Journal*, in Herb's name. He could no longer depend on occasional tearsheets, especially since Sam Algood ran the clipping service. As owner of a ball club he had to keep track of its progress day by day for the first signs of impending doom. He had to have *all* the news.

16

$ $ $

SAM WAS RIGHT. LITTLE LEAGUE RIVALED BIG LEAGUE IN THE Corinth newspapers. Whatever Pat and Scotty were doing at the gym was crowded off the pages by coverage of community sandlots. Larry had never before been aware of the number of Little League fields, complete with grandstands and fences, such as he saw pictured in the *Corinthian* and the *Evening Journal*. Both papers dutifully made the rounds, giving impartial treatment to every diamond in town—shots of uniformed players, of crowded bleachers, of harassed umpires, of frenzied parents, of booming concession stands staffed by mothers.

By the time the courtesy coverage was complete, the teams were halfway through the season. When pictures began to give way to box scores and league standings, the Federals were way out in front in their league, with six wins to only two losses. Larry was somewhat dubious of the validity of the statistics, knowing as he did that the other teams in Federals' league were from the same slum area and probably managed and coached by no more reliable characters than Sam Algood and Red Holloway.

"Federals" had long since been cut to "Feds" in captions and in the brief accounts of the games. The kids' names sounded like Big League line-ups—Polish, Italian, Czech, Latin-American, Irish. Pictures showed no color separation. Only occasionally was there a story by a regular sportswriter, however; the reporting generally bore the same amateur stamp as the games themselves. Only when Larry recognized the work of an old pro, who had probably provided a Federal uniform, did he detect the note of pride and restrained enthusiasm that marked the stories written about teams in more prosperous areas with their own reasonably literate reporters.

The Feds lost no more games during the regular season, but came to the championship play-offs with a thirteen-two record, the best of all the contenders'. Like Larry, the amateur commentators refused to consider the statistics of any real significance. For the first time the Feds would be facing solid citizens, league champions from substantial middle-class neighborhoods and from suburbia—Sylvan Heights, Rivercrest, and Sherwood Park.

When the play-offs began, about the middle of July, Larry found himself racing Katy for the Corinth papers. "Damn it, Larry, don't take so long," she would say if he got the paper first. "How did the Feds come out?"

They continued to win. The Feds started out making friends early. The various league champions, of course, were thoroughly hated by their defeated rivals, players and parents alike. Nothing could have pleased the Sylvan Heights fans more than to see the Sherwood Park champions humiliated by the little ragamuffins from the laundry. So it went. Already the protégés of the professional sportswriters, who did cover the play-offs in the minor-league ballparks, the Feds endeared themselves to the supporters of all the previously eliminated teams; and by the time they emerged as city champions they were the darlings of all Corinth.

With the announcement of a victory celebration for the Feds, Larry's heart sank. He could see the coach and manager going on a binge. He was so disturbed that he had Katy put in a call to Scotty.

He took over as soon as the call was completed.

"Congratulations, Scotty," he said. "Your team came through with flying colors."

"It isn't my team, Mr. Shelton. Red and Sam ran the whole show."

"That's really why I called," Larry said. "Can those two be trusted to attend the victory celebration?"

"Oh, sure," Scotty said confidently. "We had to sober them both up after those two defeats early in the season, but they can take victory O.K."

"I guess it's a good thing the Feds had such a good season, then."

"It sure is." Scotty chuckled. "If the team had lost, Red and Sam would have gone to hell."

"O.K.," Larry said, not completely relieved. "But you and Pat keep your eyes open."

"We will."

Larry did not rest easy, however, until he received the issue of the *Corinthian* which carried coverage of the celebration, an outdoor affair, and saw pictures of Red and Sam with the team—drinking Pepsi-Cola. In the accompanying story the Federal Physical Fitness Foundation was highly praised for the fine work it had done in giving Corinth a winning ball club from the least likely part of the city. Pat and Scotty were given credit along with the Feds' coach and manager. The value of year-round physical training, provided only for the underprivileged by the Federal program, was abundantly

117

proved by the outcome of the Little League play-offs—so the article said.

Right on cue, Letters to the Editor played variations on the same themes. One letter asked why only the underprivileged children were given full-time physical training. Why could not a city the size of Corinth look after the health of *all* its children? Another, mistaking the foundation for a federal agency, saw in it full vindication of the President's views on national health, but wondered, too, why the program was restricted to slum areas.

The Federals were sent to the national Little League play-offs in August, but were eliminated after winning their first two games. In September, while the United Fund drive filled the papers, Letters to the Editor continued to mention the need for a city-wide physical-fitness program. Some urged the United Fund to take it on; others suggested federal grants. Very discreetly a few of them mentioned a public gymnasium for Corinth, and hinted at the possibility of a local committee to look into ways of financing it. At the close of the drive, one letter pointed out the yawning gap still apparent in community services—inadequate physical-training facilities for the youth of Corinth. "The job is only partially completed. Corinth has shown the will by giving generously to the United Fund. Corinth still has money to give—to finish the job," the letter concluded.

The very next issue of the *Corinthian* announced the first meeting of the Physical Fitness Council of Corinth. Larry recognized the names of the leaders as names which had figured minutely in various activities of the United Fund. Miss Patricia Hayden and Mr. Angus (Scotty) MacGregor, whose outstanding work was familiar to everyone in Corinth, had been called in as professional advisers to the council. They had responded enthusiastically and had been received enthusiastically when they pledged full support of the Federal Fitness Foundation, at both local and national levels, in helping Corinth do

118

its share in implementing the President's physical-fitness program.

Things started jumping after that announcement. At its second meeting the council decided that a professional fund-raising agency should be called in to direct a campaign. Miss Hayden recommended a community-funds consultant with whom she had once worked in a highly successful drive. The council empowered her to contact his firm to see if he was available. She would report at the next meeting and if possible bring the fund-raiser with her. The council preferred not to release the name of the agency until its services were assured.

So Larry received his first official communication from Pat, a very formal request outlining the project and urging him to come to Corinth and lend his aid to the Physical Fitness Council.

In the same mail, he received a bulky file from Sam Algood. Since it was not likely to be revealed as an official communication, the cover letter began:

Dear BTO:

Here are your patsies.

Stanley Hogan—a Boy Scout executive, a real Boy Scout, immature, likable, tireless, gullible, and pleasantly stupid.

Miss Fanny Hill—(Don't jump to conclusions.) Spinster, rich, stingy; gives all her time to charity to salve her conscience for never giving any of her money to anything. Knows all the bigwigs and fears none of them.

Miss Helen Boatwright—Dutch bob, mannish figure, wild eyes, intense. Mention the President or one of his projects, and she flips.

Dr. (Ed. D.) J. C. Rankin—ex-public-school administrator considered unemployable because he thinks too much about what is good for the kids and not enough about what is good for the system.

Mrs. John D. Milliken—reputedly frigid matron who di-

rects her attention to community projects lest it comes to focus on her husband's philandering.

Mr. Charlie Shanks—past president of the Optimists, still an optimist.

Mrs. Dora Mansfield—wealthy widow. Right now it's your gymnasium. Last year it was progressive jazz; the year before, theosophy.

They tell me seven is a good number for a committee. These are not all stupid old biddies by any means, but they are safe and they are malleable. Two more might have brought in a dissenter. Pat and Scotty seem to have everything under control pending your arrival.

Handle the envelope marked CONFIDENTIAL with care.

Yours for the health of the nation,

J. Samuel Algood

Larry broke the seal on the fat envelope marked CONFIDENTIAL. It contained a complete list of United Fund contributors, carefully annotated in the upper brackets. In addition there were other lists of known philanthropists who held aversions to the United Fund but who had good giving records to various causes.

Last of all was a note from Sam:

This will cost somebody—you or the council or the foundation—an even grand. The informer, being an old crony of mine, put it on the cuff. Whose cuff I wouldn't know; but somebody had better damn sure claim the shirt.

Good old Sam was developing into a highly successful fund raiser—five thousand for himself, five hundred for Red Holloway, and now another thousand for some anonymous old crony who snitched subscription lists. He might prove an invaluable Associate if he ever started soliciting funds *for* Larry instead of *from* him. Well, the time had come for the switch. The fish had taken the lure. Larry could now play the hunter, stalk his prey, and gun it down. He started assembling the campaign aids he would need there. He went through his files for posters, fliers, pledge cards, tally sheets, news releases, form letters—all the various items which would serve as patterns for matter to be printed in Corinth by Corinthians. He called a balloon manufacturer and placed a special order in layaway, for immediate delivery when the time came. Then he made sure that an assortment of buttons, hats, arm bands, and other such paraphernalia would be available for rush orders.

All the suppliers knew him from former campaigns, and promised quick service on demand. When he made a final survey of his check list, he felt confident that he had everything lined up for a whirlwind drive—everything except what awaited him in Corinth. And on the third Sunday in October he caught a plane to find out what that was.

17

$ $ $

"THE ACRO-CORINTHUS HOTEL," LARRY SAID TO THE TAXI DRIVER as a skycap loaded his luggage into the trunk.

"The Acro it is, Mister."

Larry made a mental note. The Acro it would be henceforth. He settled back into his seat and correlated the business signs along the route into town with the donor lists Sam had sent him. He already had the upper levels pretty well memorized, and categorized into Solid Citizens ($100 to $1,000), Big Boys ($1,000 to $10,000), and Golden Givers ($10,000 +). All part of his training.

At the Acro he asked for the suite he had reserved by wire.

"Yes, sir, Mr. Shelton, we were able to hold it for you," the desk clerk informed him. "How long will you be staying with us?"

"I'll be here at least a week, possibly six weeks. I'll let you know before Saturday."

"I hope you'll be with us the whole time, sir."

"So do I," Larry said, and turned to follow the bellboy who had taken his key.

Suite 312 was more than adequate, a spacious sitting room big enough for conferences, and a large, comfortable bedroom. Recently redecorated, the rooms were still very consciously Greek in décor, with statues and friezes and false columns principally Doric and Ionic in conception.

Larry unpacked casually and put away his clothes for a long stay. About four o'clock he called Pat Hayden.

"Oh, Larry," Pat answered eagerly, "why didn't you tell us when you were arriving? We would have met your plane."

"I wouldn't think of disturbing your day of rest—not before dinnertime, anyway. Are you booked for this evening?"

"No—" Was there hesitancy in her voice?

"If not, I'd like to get you and Scotty and Sam together —say at Angelo's?"

"That would be fine. I'll collect them and pick you up. About when?"

"Oh, about six, if you can make it."

"We can make it. The Acro, I suppose."

The "we" gave Larry a little worry while he was bathing and dressing. He could not tell just how much of his eagerness to come to Corinth had been prompted by business and how much by the possibility of seeing Pat again.

The pictures of her in the newspapers had appeared quite provocative to him—to all male readers, he admitted, and chuckled in the shower. "We" obviously included Scotty, and probably Sam, even Red Holloway and whoever else had been working with her. Pat was co-operative, a selfless team member. He was justifiably happy to be working with her on another campaign. Only, this time it would be different during the drive—and after?

Scotty came into the lobby for him and showed him to the car, where he opened the front door for Larry and crawled into the back beside Sam. It was the same car, the same Pat who had chauffered Larry during the Calvary Church campaign.

"It's so good to see you, Larry," Pat said. "Everyone is so enthusiastic and so eager to get started. I've told them all about you."

Not *all*, Larry was sure. He glanced sidelong at her—the same fall coat she had worn in New York.

"You've got a lot to live up to, BTO," Sam said from the back seat. "I'm the only one who doesn't believe the build-up your little pigeon has given you."

"Unfavorable press," Larry commented. "That's the way with you cynics. You won't admit greatness when you see it."

"I'm still to see it," Sam said genially.

"You'll see it," Pat assured him.

At Angelo's it became apparent that the trio were habitués. Angelo frowned momentarily, as though he should remember Larry from somewhere; but Momma's effusive greeting to Pat and the others reassured Larry that the girl could do no wrong. So any secret the family might deduce would stay in the family.

The steaks were wonderful, as tender as your beloved. The conspirators lingered long over their coffee.

"Sam, I'll want you to spend tomorrow with me, going over some lists," Larry said.

"Sure." Sam grinned.

123

"What time will you and Scotty be free, Pat?"

"By five."

"Good. There's a lot of confidential typing to be done right away. I'll have a typewriter sent up to my room."

"I can bring a portable," she said. "But you are coming out to see the gym, aren't you?"

"Yes, sometime tomorrow afternoon. We'll take a break."

"I think you'll be surprised." Then she frowned. "Larry, isn't there something you can do for Red? He's been our janitor since the baseball season closed. He loves the kids so, and they love him. He hasn't needed any money."

"Hell, I've been supporting him," Sam said, trying hard to make his words sound like a complaint.

"Couldn't Mr. Phillips—I mean the foundation—pay him a little?" Pat asked.

"Why you chiselers, you panhandlers, you—"

"Fund raisers," Sam said with a guffaw. In the dim light he looked as healthy as Pat and Scotty—almost.

"Write Herb and ask him," Larry said, going down in defeat.

In the bright morning light Sam still looked healthy. His face and frame were lean, but no longer gaunt. He was clean-shaven, and the red streaks of dawn had faded from his mist-gray eyes. His casual tweed suit fitted about as well as any suit ever fitted a newshound.

"You remind me vaguely of a baseball player," Larry said when he showed Sam to a chair.

"In college I was vaguely a baseball player," Sam admitted. "Vaguely an outfielder and more vaguely a pitcher."

"You boys did all right with the Feds."

"The kids did all right, you mean. They did a lot for me and Red, too," Sam said soberly. "Thanks for taking Red on, BTO. You just might have snatched him back from hell."

"On your judgment, Sam. I hope it's as good on these guys." Larry laid the donor lists on a table beside Sam. "I've checked them with colored pencils. Red, good for a hundred bucks and up. Blue, good for a thousand or more. Orange, ten thousand plus. I'm going on their records. You may know some of them, by reputation at least, especially the Blue Chips and the Golden Givers?"

"Sure. I can help some."

For three hours Sam evaluated prospects and gave background information while Larry took notes. The newspaper man was full of facts, rumors, gossip, and no small measure of spleen, all of which were invaluable to a fund raiser. Larry could not have opened a richer vein in his gold mine.

Next, Larry turned to the Physical Fitness Council of Corinth for a similar rundown.

"Who's my door opener?" he asked. "Who can get me into the top offices of industry and management?"

"Miss Fanny. Old family. Her father backed half the successful businessmen in this town and made it hell for the other half. She can get you in if anyone can."

"O.K. Who knows the Golden Givers, the independently wealthy?"

"The country-club crowd? Dora Mansfield. She knows them all socially and has slept with a goodly number of them."

"Fine. Service clubs?"

"Charlie Shanks, the perennial optimist."

"I guessed as much," Larry said. "Now for the women's clubs?"

"Mrs. Milliken—Claire, I believe her name is. She is always billed as Mrs. John D., but in name only, I suspect."

"Medium bracket? Solid Citizens who have come up the hard way."

"Old Dr. Rankin, a latter-day Mr. Chips. He got them out of scrapes and lent a helping hand while he was superintendent of schools. They're still grateful—most of them."

"Fine. Stanley Hogan seems to be the hoopla boy," Larry said. "What's Helen Boatwright good for?"

"Welfare wishers and intellectuals. I know, they never give anything; but they're vocal. I thought they might help."

"Right you are," Larry agreed. "Now. Who heads these drives? Mayor Hopkins headed the United Fund. Was that honorary?"

"Partially." Sam frowned. "He heads everything. And there's your snag. He doesn't like your gymnasium idea worth a damn."

"Why not?"

"It's going to cost a million bucks, and it's coming out of a fund he can't dip into. What reason he'll give officially I don't know."

"O.K. He's our Campaign Chairman."

"Want to bet?" Sam's lips grinned beneath level poker eyes.

"Hell, I've bet almost fifty grand already. I'm not folding this hand. Name your stakes."

"Next week's salary. And I personally think it will be my last paycheck. You can't put this over without Big Jack Hopkins, and you'll never get His Honor on your team."

"What are his politics?"

"Liberal Democrat in name, machine in fact. You haven't got a chance."

"You're called," Larry said. "Let's have lunch and go pay the kids a visit."

Larry recognized the street, but the building did come as a surprise. The front was painted fresh and bright, and the grounds were well kept. Passing through the entrance with Sam, he saw open doors on each side into immaculate little offices, one Pat's, one Scotty's. The employees' shower and dressing rooms were marked BOYS and GIRLS.

"I see that Pat let them paint the inside walls after all," Larry said.

"Water-soluble paint," Sam said, obviously conversant with the problem. "Nary a stench, nary a bellyache."

Entering the gym proper, Larry saw first (as anyone would have seen first) Pat in a full-length leotard, tumbling with a dozen pre-school misses. She looked exactly like what the man had in mind when he invented the leotard.

"We've learned not to whistle," Sam said softly, as Pat announced a recess and came toward them. As for self-consciousness, she might as well have been wearing hooped crinoline and pantalets.

"We were expecting you," Pat said, extending her hand.

"We" meant the preschoolers, who swarmed over Sam, squealing like sub-Beatle fans. Obviously he had not devoted all his time to the baseball team.

"How do you like it?" Pat asked proudly.

"Remarkable."

"We've had lots of free help."

"You must have."

"Parents and so on. They're as proud of the place as we are."

"They should be." Larry trailed a hand in the swimming pool as Pat led him to the rear of the gym, where Scotty was refereeing a volleyball game between mites scarcely bigger than the ball.

"The water's a little cool. We swim on Tuesdays and Thursdays. It'll be warm in the morning," Pat said.

Scotty saw them and started their way. He had hardly looked at Pat, either because of complete lack of interest or because of excessive familiarity. Larry wondered which. He could not imagine being near Pat and not being aware of her.

"Well, Mr. Shelton, what do you think?" Scotty asked, timorously, as though he expected some complaint.

"Remarkable, as I said to Pat." These crazy kids still had their eyes on the gym—this gym. "You've done all we expected," Larry said, but went on to remind them, "Our real job starts tomorrow, raising funds for the new gymnasium."

"I can hardly wait," Pat said, and Larry thought he detected the note of avidity with which she had spoken of Calvary Church. He hoped so.

"I suppose you have arranged it so you can help at Campaign Headquarters," Larry said to her.

"Oh, yes, in the mornings," Pat said. "I have a vocational nurse who will come in then. I'll combine the calisthenics classes and meet them at two. Scotty and I will have to take the schoolchildren at their regular hours—three and four. But we'll be available again for nightwork."

She spoke for Scotty very authoritatively, Larry noted. There was no question about who ran the place. She was going to make a first-class Associate when he brought her into the Home Office.

"Here's Red," she said abruptly, as a shadow slunk out of the boiler room. "Mr. Holloway, this is Mr. Shelton."

"Hi, Red," Larry said, extending his hand.

"Hello, Mr. Shelton. Glad to know you." But Red's hands already had an ex-volleyball player hanging on each finger.

"I've told Red he's on salary now," Pat said, smiling indulgently at the shadow. This was the crew that was going to make or break Laurence P. Shelton Associates—in a hurry.

"Yeah. Thanks, Mr. Shelton."

"You did a fine job with the Feds," Larry said, not grudgingly he hoped.

"Yeah," Red said, brightening. "Them kids was sure in there hustling all season."

"I have another hustling job coming up for you and Scotty," Larry said. By God, everybody on salary was going to work—for him.

"What's that?" Scotty asked.

"Lining up my All-Stars."

"All-Stars?" Scotty asked. "Who are they?"

"They're all the name athletes in Corinth. Big names, little names. All the pro, college, or high-school heroes, exes, who have ever been heard of. I want them organized and set to hustling money at all the high-school football games in town for the next month. Do you know them?"

"Some of them," Scotty said.

"Me, too. Some of them," Red echoed.

"And each one knows one, or two, or three. So that's a job for you two heroes. Recruit every one you can find."

Both heroes grinned and nodded.

Just then a stampede through the front door marked the end of that session and the start of the next.

"Back to your foolishness," Larry said to the athletic directors, and sought refuge against the front wall.

He and Sam watched for half an hour or more. It was interesting to watch Scotty, fascinating to watch Pat. Red had disappeared.

"We've got work to do," Larry reminded his companion. "I suppose you know some printers around town."

"Sure."

"Well, come on back to the hotel with me. I have some forms to be printed up on short notice. You can help me revise them to fit this campaign."

"O.K. I'll go along with you until you stall. You hired me." They went to call a taxi.

"You wouldn't try to hedge your bet, would you, Sam?"

"Look, there's nothing I'd rather do than lose next week's salary to you," Sam said earnestly. "But I don't think you've got a prayer—not against Big Jack Hopkins. In him you'll meet your match."

Back at the hotel, the two wrote copy for campaign literature. Sam, who knew his type faces and composition, annotated for format.

By the time Pat and Scotty arrived, they had everything ready for typing. Larry had another typewriter sent in and put Sam to work helping her.

He and Scotty went through the donor lists and sorted out sublists according to color code, to be retyped without headings of any kind. Sometime after midnight the material was ready for printing or duplicating.

"When do I deliver these to the printers?" Sam asked, collecting his copy.

"When Mayor Hopkins agrees to head the drive."

"Haw, haw, haw," Sam said.

"Before the end of the week," Larry promised.

"And haw, haw, haw, again. Calling your shots."

"Eight ball in the side pocket, one bank."

Pat and Scotty listened to the interplay with bewildered expressions.

"A private joke," Larry said, and they smiled halfheartedly. "I'll have copies of these lists ready for the council meeting tomorrow night. And thanks to you, Pat—and to you, Scotty—for helping out."

Both looked tired when they left Suite 312. Larry shuddered at the thought of the strenuous exercise they had to face the next morning.

18

$ $ $

DURING THE DAY PAT CALLED ALL MEMBERS OF THE PHYSICAL Fitness Council to change the meeting place to Suite 312, and was on hand at seven o'clock to introduce them to Larry, who, however, would have recognized them immediately from Sam's thumbnail sketches. He might have mistaken Dora Mansfield for Claire Milliken, or vice versa. Both were younger than he had expected—in the neighborhod of thirty—but of a type he knew well from former campaigns, women with unsatisfactory home lives, or none at all, whiling away the hours, waiting—but not stupid old biddies by any means. Both looked expensive, and worth the price.

Helen Boatwright was a few years older, ineffectually intense, acquiescent to discipline, veteran of a long line of lost causes, a born jinx to poorly organized ventures. Miss Fanny Hill was pushing seventy, but pushing it with a wiry, waspish will that was sure to make it yield.

"Don't call me Miss Hill, young man," she said to Larry. "That was my elder sister Grace. I'm Miss Fanny."

"Glad to know you, Miss Fanny."

Charlie Shanks would have slapped Larry on the back but for the presence of Pat in the line of travel. Dr. Rankin took Larry's hand gently but firmly and welcomed him to Corinth in an effortless bass voice. Stanley Hogan was big, not fat, but rather soft of muscle, and boyish in his actions, a lovable mutt who might enjoy the hunt even though he would most likely be off chasing rabbits at the moment of the kill.

So Larry catalogued the council as they sat down around the portable banquet table he had set up in his sitting room. He and Sam sat on a sofa while Stanley Hogan, as president of the council, called the meeting to order and Helen Boatwright read the minutes of the last meeting.

"We are happy that Miss Hayden has fulfilled the last order of business and brought Mr. Shelton to this meeting," Hogan said after the minutes had been read and approved.

"We have no financial report," he added apologetically. "In fact, we have no finances, Mr. Shelton." He laughed self-consciously.

"That's my business," Larry said, since the remark had been addressed specifically to him.

"And we sincerely hope you will handle it. I believe I speak for the entire council."

The entire council nodded.

"That is our sole order of business for this evening," Hogan said, still standing, as a chairman should stand according to Robert. "I trust Miss Hayden has outlined our project for you."

"In detail," Larry said. "I believe I have the picture."

"Well, what do you think?" The president sat down, obviously inviting Larry to take the floor.

"I would say that the prospects are good," Larry said, rising. "Provided, of course, that we get the wholehearted support of the community. By that, I mean a campaign committee of stature in Corinth—hundreds of people just like you, dedicated and energetic—with a chairman who will alert all the citizens of Corinth to the need for a gymnasium and make them aware of the opportunity to give the gym reality. You members of this council naturally know more about the possibility of recruiting such an organization than I do.

"My office has mined its resources for pertinent information, which I have with me; but in the final analysis it will be you—the pioneers in this project—who will provide our work force. I should like to hear some of your suggestions before I commit myself." Larry left an opening for the chairman to speak again.

"Well," Hogan began uncertainly, "we have discussed the matter, of course; but we haven't come up with anything concrete. Uh—uh—we thought—that is, Miss Hayden led us to believe that you—that you—"

"That's exactly what we called you in for, young man," Miss Fanny reminded Larry. "I believe you call yourself a consultant on community funds. If we're to handle it ourselves, just what is your job? What do you do to earn your fee?"

"I am consulting with you, Miss Fanny," Larry said with no argumentative intonation. "This council has done a superb job of ground breaking. You really can't blame me for getting you to do as much of my work for me as possible, can you?" He grinned sheepishly at her, as though she had caught him picking her peonies.

"Well, let me consult with you for a moment," Miss

132

Fanny said, mollified to some extent. "What has your office come up with so far?"

"My research staff made a quick study of former campaigns held in Corinth and came up with one man who seems to have headed most of them—Mayor Hopkins."

"Humph!" Miss Fanny voiced the deflation of the entire council.

"That's the hitch," Stanley Hogan said uncomfortably. "We've approached him, not to ask his help, but to explain our plans to him. He refuses to see us as a committee."

"But he would be the man?" Larry asked, as though defending his research staff's findings.

"Oh, yes," Dr. Rankin spoke up, naïvely perhaps. "Jack Hopkins would be our biggest asset in a city-wide campaign."

"Then we must try again," Larry said confidently. "We should call on him first thing in the morning."

"He won't even talk to us," Hogan said. "We can't get an appointment."

"Who knows him best?" Larry asked.

"Dora," Mrs. Milliken said, somewhat maliciously.

"Yes, I know Jack," Dora said.

"Would you call him for us?" Larry asked.

"The City Council meets on Tuesdays, at eight," Sam Algood volunteered. "He's probably in his office right now. You might get him before the meeting begins." Sam was looking at Larry, needling him.

"Will you try, Mrs. Mansfield?" Larry asked.

"Yes—yes, I'll try," she said hesitantly.

Larry showed her to his telephone, and the council was quiet while Dora Mansfield called outside and finally got the mayor on the telephone without revealing any more than her name to the various operators and secretaries.

"Jack?" she said at last. "Yes. This is Dora Mansfield. I'm at the Acro."

She laughed, a little guiltily, and then went on: "I'm calling on behalf of the Physical Fitness Council of Corinth. We were wondering if you could meet with us in the morning."

There was a lull in the conversation from Dora's end of the line. She frowned and shook her head in the direction of the listening council.

"Tell him we are preparing a press release covering this meeting," Larry coached Dora softly. "Tell him we would like to include the announcement of an appointment with him."

When she had an opening, Dora relayed Larry's message. She covered the mouthpiece with her right hand and whispered, "He still says no."

"Then we'll have to include his refusal in the news release."

Dora repeated that information, with a note of glee in her voice.

After another lull, she brightened.

"At ten, then, Jack?" she asked. "O.K. We'll be there at ten."

"Neat," she said, smiling up at Larry as she cradled the telephone.

"That's that," Larry said to the council. "We have an appointment with the mayor at ten o'clock in the morning." He looked at no one directly, not even at Sam.

"Thank you for calling, Mrs. Mansfield," he said, escorting her back to her seat at the council table.

"It was a pleasure," she said. "I wouldn't miss tomorrow's meeting for anything."

"Will you take on our campaign, Mr. Shelton?" Stanley Hogan blurted out. He was still uneasy. "I mean we'd like some kind of contract before we proceed any further. Isn't that the will of this body?" He belatedly looked around for support. The council nodded and voiced approval variously.

"Yes, I think I can assure you that my firm will conduct the drive for you. However, I would rather not sign a con-

134

tract until I am sure of the campaign committee and chairman. Do you have any other nominations for chairman?"

"I'm sure we can find someone," Helen Boatwright said, desperately, hedging against another losing cause.

"There are lots of fine men in Corinth," Charlie Shanks said. "I know dozens of go-getters in this town."

"Jack Hopkins is our best prospect," Dr. Rankin insisted.

"I am inclined to agree with Dr. Rankin," Larry said. "And I certainly hope we can get the mayor's consent to head our drive. I do have a rather extensive file prepared by my staff, however. I would like each of you to look over some lists for likely members of the campaign committee and for volunteer workers."

Larry took the selective lists from his desk and passed them around, each to the council member most likely to be familiar with the various graduated gift brackets. He noted some surprised expressions as the members glanced over the mimeographed sheets.

"Your staff seems to be quite efficient, young man," Miss Fanny commented.

"We try to be," Larry said. "If each of you will study these lists and suggest some good people—the best you can think of, whether or not you find their names included—for campaign workers, we might be able to help the mayor choose his committee when we meet with him in the morning."

A steady hum began around the council table, comparisons of ideas, little sounds of pleasure at the recognition of names, questions, answers, expressions of approval of the initial thoroughness of Laurence P. Shelton Associates. By the time the meeting broke up, Larry was satisfied with the balance of enthusiasm and anxiety he had generated in the council.

Sam called in the press release and insured coverage of the next morning's meeting before he left Suite 312.

Larry lulled himself to sleep going over in his memory every detail of the evening's activities. When he awoke, he

135

reviewed the proceedings again so that he felt confidence in himself and in the council when he met them in a vacant courtroom in the city hall a few minutes before ten on Wednesday. He noted the reporters seated at the press table as he joined Stanley Hogan and Helen Boatwright at a smaller table usually reserved for the defense attorneys when court was in session. The rest of the council sat outside the railing, in auditorium seats.

"All set?" Larry asked as he sat down .

"Well, I've prepared a presentation speech," Hogan said. "Helen has some notes and statistics to back me up if I need them."

"Fine," Larry said, opening his own brief case and spreading a few papers before him to make his presence look official.

He was still busy when the mayor, a big well-fed florid politician, appeared through a door from the judge's chambers. Larry appreciated his entry, a solemn spectacle calculated to intimidate the petitioners. Larry would not have been surprised if His Honor had worn a robe. He half expected the council to rise.

"Good morning," the mayor said in a booming voice of forced geniality.

Everyone else mumbled.

"I believe this is the Physical Fitness Council of Corinth," the mayor said as he sat down on the judge's bench. "I recognize most of you as old friends. Who is your spokesman?"

"I am, Your Honor," Stanley Hogan said, rising.

"Oh, yes, Stan. Good to see you. Just what do you have in mind?"

Stanley Hogan rendered his presentation speech, sometimes haltingly, always apologetically. Obviously he was more at home at Boy Scout jamborees.

"And so, Your Honor, we'd like your help in this campaign," Stan ended lamely.

"Well, Stan, you and I have worked together in scouting for a number of years. You know I've always been a booster, always interested in the welfare of the boys and girls of Corinth.

"And I think we've done right well by them—lots of parks, swimming pools, a fine Little League program. I'll tell you, Stan, I just don't believe we need a public gymnasium right now."

"Those Little League champions came right out of a year-round charity gymnasium program," Helen Boatwright reminded the mayor. She did not stand. She was trembling so that Larry doubted that she could have stood.

"Ah, yes, yes. Fine work that group is doing over there in the old laundry. Proves my point. We're doing all right by our kids."

"Only a minute portion of them," Helen managed to say. She was about used up.

"We need facilities for *all* of them, Jack Hopkins," Miss Fanny piped up from the spectators' section.

"Oh, Miss Fanny. I didn't see you at first. How are you this morning?"

"Getting impatient. Don't try to change the subject. Let's get together and build this gym."

"Now, now, Miss Fanny. You know as well as I do all the things we're doing in Corinth. This new city hall, the new civic center. We don't want to have to raise any tax rates in this town."

"There's no tax money involved in this project, Jack." Dr. Rankin spoke softly, but his voice carried well throughout the room. "We plan to build it entirely by voluntary contributions."

"Dr. Rankin! It's been a long time, hasn't it? You're looking well."

"Feeling fit, too, Jack. Still interested in kids."

"You always were, Doc. You helped us build one of the finest school systems in the state. We have excellent athletic programs in our schools, too, which you helped develop. I'm

137

sure you'll agree with me that we are taking care of the physical training of our public-school students."

"Of a handful of natural-born athletes in each school," Dr. Rankin admitted. "But hardly touching the rest. No, Jack, I don't agree with you. We need a public gymnasium; and with your help, we can build it."

"Now, now, Doc, let's be practical. A million dollars is a lot of money. Maybe, someday, we'll need such a facility. Maybe, someday, there will be money available to build it. But I think your project is premature and ill-advised. Just how do you think you're going to raise a million dollars?" The edge in the mayor's voice was getting keener. His color was rising.

"Just as I said," Dr. Rankin went on calmly. "By voluntary contributions, by public subscription. We can do it."

"And just who are we?"

"You, Jack, and me—the members of this council, all the public-spirited people in Corinth. With you heading our drive—"

"With me heading your drive?" The mayor burst out laughing. "Why, I haven't the time or the—"

Larry jumped up and began to repack his brief case angrily and noisily.

"Who are you?" the mayor roared. "And what are you doing?"

"I'm a consultant called in by this council," Larry roared back at him. "And I'm packing up to leave. I came here in good faith to help these poor impractical idealists do something for the kids of Corinth. But I've been misled and misinformed. I have no intention of forcing myself on a city administration that doesn't need, doesn't want, and doesn't intend to build a public gymnasium for its youth."

Without giving the mayor a chance to interrupt, Larry slammed his brief case shut and turned to face the press table.

He said, loud and clear, "There are your afternoon headlines, gentleman:

138

MAYOR OPPOSES PRESIDENT'S PHYSICAL FITNESS PROGRAM
TURNS THUMBS DOWN ON FEDERAL GYMNASIUM
LAUGHS IN THE FACES OF THE COUNCIL

I've heard enough."

He turned, stalked toward the railing, and opened the gate. He was halfway down the center aisle before Big Jack recovered his voice.

"Hey, you," the mayor yelled. "Come back here. I didn't say any such thing. Let's set the record straight."

"What do you mean, 'set the record straight'?" Larry asked, turning his head only far enough for him to see the mayor. "I heard you. I'm not deaf, you know, and I don't live in Corinth. I don't owe you or your city a damn thing."

"Come on back and let's talk this over." The mayor was bordering on apoplexy, but he had his voice under control.

"What is there to talk over?" Larry turned his body around but made no move to return to the front of the courtroom.

"Stan's proposal." The mayor was trying hard. "Stan, how much time do you think I would have to give to your drive?"

"Uh—uh—not much, Your Honor." Stan swallowed twice. "Just endorse our campaign—let us use your name—declare November 'Physical Fitness Month'—little things like that. We'll do all the work."

"That's not so much. Maybe we can get together after all. Let's be calm about this."

As Larry walked back down the aisle he glanced over at Sam Algood who stood by the press table, unobtrusively turning his pants pockets inside out.

19

$ $ $

"I HAD TO TALK TO YOU ALONE BEFORE THE OTHERS GOT HERE," Pat Hayden said by way of explaining her arrival at Suite 312 a few minutes before nine on Thursday morning.

"Come right in," Larry said. "I have everything ready for the meeting."

She remained standing after he had closed the door. Her worried look was as becoming as her usual good-natured smile. She looked chic in her new fall outfit, and she smelled good.

"You frighten me, Larry," she began.

"How? Why?"

"I've never seen you angry before. I worried all night. Would you really have walked out on us yesterday? I mean at the city hall?"

Larry laughed.

"I didn't have to," he said. "The mayor came around all right."

"I know. But really—if you get angry again, will you pull out on us? Can we depend on you? Would you desert us in this campaign?"

"Desert whom?" Larry looked at her in astonishment. "My God, Pat. Have you forgotten who set this all up? Do you remember who the Federal Physical Fitness Foundation

140

is? Just about every penny I have is tied up in this thing—I can't quit."

"Sometimes I guess I do forget." She walked over and looked out a window. "It all seems so real—the laundry, the kids, all the good we're—you're doing."

"Well, it isn't real," Larry said brutally. "It's all a money hunter's gimmick. I put on an act for the mayor, Pat, *an act*, one of the oldest tricks in the bag. And it worked."

"Yes, it worked, and I'm glad." She looked up at him, smiling uncertainly.

"You can expect a good many more." His body was almost touching hers. "Look, Pat, I may have to deceive a lot of people one way or another before this campaign is over— lie, cheat, bully, cajole, blackmail—all sorts of ways. But I don't want you to be deceived by anything I do. I want you to understand exactly what I'm doing and why I'm doing it. See?"

She nodded.

"I never want to mislead you," he went on carefully. "I want you to see me exactly as I am because—well, because you're something pretty special for me."

"And you're something pretty extra, extra special for me, if you believe me," she said—ruefully, he thought.

"I believe you—but that was not what I meant."

"Nor all I meant, either," Pat said.

A knock at the door interrupted the conversation.

"I'll get it," Pat said, the efficient headquarters girl again.

But she did not get it, not what Larry meant. He was not sure himself what he meant. Pat stood for something good. She was the measure of his morality. She had to understand what he was doing and why. And she had to approve. Then—

"Hi, Larry." It was Stan, first-naming him from the doorway.

"Hi, Stan. All set?"

"Yes, sirree. I spent all yesterday afternoon with one of the mayor's secretaries. Jack practically let me name his committee—all the people chosen by the council—and we sent out letters to every one of them on his stationery, over his signature."

"Fine, Stan. I was sure that he would lend us a hand."

"Well, I didn't actually see him again. He just told us to go ahead and left it to us. Big Jack is an all-right guy."

"He sure is," Larry agreed. "Well, your next job is organizing the parade for Saturday, November second. I suppose you've been thinking about that."

"Sure as shooting. I guess my boys have been in every parade in Corinth for the last ten years. I was marshal a couple of years ago. I know all the band directors, the Legion commanders, the drill teams—everybody. We'll have a wingding of a parade."

"That's what I expect of you, Stan. I've already wired New York suppliers for the special paraphernalia we'll need for this one. The stuff will be here in time."

Dora Mansfield and Claire Milliken arrived within a minute or two of each other, and Miss Fanny and Helen Boatwright came a little later. Dr. Rankin was last to arrive. Charlie Shanks had to work that morning.

"Why don't you just take over from here, Larry?" Stanley Hogan suggested after the meeting had been called to order. "All this must be old hat to you."

"I can, of course, offer some suggestions," Larry agreed. "I'll be happy to, if it is the will of this body."

It was the will of the body.

"O.K.," Larry went on. "I have organization charts here with sixteen categories of workers, from those who will gain entrée to the Golden Givers down to the Wind Bags—our speakers' bureau."

The council members chuckled at his latter category, and laughed aloud when they glanced over the organization charts he passed out.

"Call Girls!" Dora Mansfield exclaimed. "They ought to rake in the cash."

142

"Telephone corps," Larry explained. "And they're the first ones we'll have to recruit—to call all the others for us, and later to do solicitation by telephone."

"Bell Ringers?" Miss Fanny repeated inquiringly.

"Doorbells. House-to-house at eventide," Larry said. "The last ones to bring in nickels and dimes, the drippings—a couple for every block in town—during the final days of the campaign—Thanksgiving week."

"Roll Callers?" Claire asked.

"Union stewards. Payday roll call at industrial plants and factories."

"I know who the All-Stars are," Pat said. "Ex-athletes to work the football games."

"Right."

"Gold Diggers?" It was obvious the tack Dora Mansfield's mind was taking.

"High-school girls' drill teams, in uniform, to work shopping centers on the evenings they stay open. Just wait until you see the miners' hard hats—gold yet—and the lightweight picks I've ordered for them to use."

"Comprehensive," Dr. Rankin observed, nodding his head. "Comprehensive coverage. I'm beginning to see how you fund raisers justify your existence."

"Comprehensive if properly staffed," Larry said. "Now this council must grow like mustard seeds. I hope that you know the people, or know people who know the people, to staff every one of these committees.

"We'll need at least three hundred people, key people, here for the Kickoff Banquet on November one, and they must expand our work force to ten or fifteen thousand as the campaign progresses."

"Whew!" Helen Boatwright was obviously thinking big for the first time in her life.

"With your authorization, I'll reserve the ballroom here at the Acro for the banquet and as Campaign Headquarters from Monday next through November, if it is available."

"How much will that cost?" Stan asked.

"Five or six thousand dollars ought to cover it, banquet and all."

"Well, now, Larry, we don't have that kind of money—not yet."

"We will have in a day or two after the banquet. I believe you've arranged with the Federal Physicial Fitness Foundation to handle all your finances."

"Yes," Stan said. "Miss Hayden—Pat—put us in touch with Mr. Phillips—the president of the foundation. I believe you said you knew him."

"I talked with him before I left New York—yes," Larry said.

"Well, he agreed to let us use the foundation as our interim depository. It's chartered, you know."

"Yes, I know. A sound institution," Larry commented.

"But I'm not sure we should obligate the foundation for anything in advance."

"Miss Hayden—Pat—you're an authorized agent of the foundation, aren't you?" Larry asked.

"Yes." The caution in her answer sounded natural enough. Larry wondered if her hesitancy was prompted by unwillingness to be a party to duplicity.

"Well?"

"I could call Mr. Phillips, and ask."

"Please do."

"Now?"

"Yes. Use my telephone."

Pat, somewhat reluctantly, put in a call to Herb's office. She got him immediately and made her request, with the timidity one might expect from a lowly field worker speaking to the president.

"Yes, he's here with us," Pat said after a pause. "Would you like to speak to him? Larry—"

She handed the telephone to Larry, who was standing beside her.

144

"Hello, bastard brother-in-law," Herb said by way of greeting.

"Yes, this is Laurence P. Shelton," Larry answered.

"Con artist, swindler, fink extraordinary."

"Of course, Mr. Phillips."

"That's what I wanted to verify."

"Certainly, Mr. Phillips. Laurence P. Shelton Associates will underwrite the entire amount if the campaign does not succeed. You may prepare a sight draft on us."

"I might do just that, chiseler, and take Katy on a Caribbean cruise. Winter is acoming in up here before afore long." Herb chuckled.

"Yes, Mr. Phillips, that will be fine."

"Put Pat back on—in color TV if possible."

"Pat—" Larry returned the instrument to her.

"Hello, Mr. Phillips." She listened for a few seconds. "Yes, thank you, Mr. Phillips."

"He says it's all right," she reported to the council, but her eyes would not meet Larry's, or anyone else's.

"Then I'll go ahead with the arrangements, if it is the will of this body."

Again it was the will of the body.

"Let's see," Larry continued. "We have a roster of the Mayor's Committee. You have the organization charts with the various other committees and on the second page an explanation of the duties of each.

"If you will study those overnight and come back with suggestions for personnel, we can prepare our banquet invitation list in the morning. We'll need our Call Girls at once, too. Think of as many as you can, call them, explain our needs, and ask them to recruit others.

"I'll get two regular typists from an employment agency to work here through Sunday, and I believe Charlie Shanks can get us several more on loan from his friends to work in shifts beginning Monday.

145

"That's about all for now, I guess," Larry ended. "Except for you, Mrs. Mansfield."

"Dora," she said, smiling.

"Dora, I need some special information from you. If you are free and can stay a while, I'll buy you a lunch while I pump you."

"For a free lunch I'll reveal Cleopatra's state secrets."

"It's a deal, then."

Stanley Hogan took the chair long enough to adjourn the meeting. Pat was thoughtful as she left—almost accusing, Larry thought. Claire Milliken was last to go, wearing a wise expression which said she was loath to leave "you two" alone.

"What's the Big Question?" Dora asked, as soon as the others were gone.

"Do you take a drink before lunch?"

"I take a drink before lunch."

"Here?" Larry asked.

"Anywhere."

Larry called room service for martinis, and they both sat down on the sofa. He sighed as he sank into the cushions, but said nothing for a moment.

"Surely that's not the only question you had to ask," Dora prompted him.

"No. Who in Corinth will give me a hundred thousand dollars before next Friday night?"

"Nobody."

"Who could?"

"I could, but I won't."

"That would be too easy," Larry said, grinning at her. "I wouldn't accept that kind of money from a woman."

"Grandstanding again, huh? A big play for your co-workers at the banquet?" Dora understood him, as he thought she would.

The martinis arrived, and he left her question unanswered.

"Really, I couldn't give that much," she said at last. "Not without selling some securities. Not many people in town could. I'll name *one* who can, and I'll bet you ten thousand he won't; but he would be a feather in your cap if you could bring it off."

"Who?" Larry asked.

"Jason Hill."

"Any kin to Miss Fanny?"

"Cousin. Of course she could too, but—"

"—but I don't accept that kind of money from women."

They both laughed.

"Tell me about Jason," Larry said.

"He is sole owner, and chairman of the dummy board, of Hill Enterprises—a little bit of everything. No financial connections with Miss Fanny. She disowned him a few years ago when he married that little snippet."

"Tell me about the snippet."

"She's a little younger than I am," Dora said, "and Jason's a little older than Miss Fanny. He married her late in life—too late, I think. Anyway, they have no children, but he adores her."

"What does she do for recreation?"

"Adores old Jason. Make no mistake about that."

"Who has hopes?"

"Tom Bradford, president of Hill Enterprises, but an out-and-out hired man—not a single share of stock."

"How old?"

"Forty, I would say."

"Huh," Larry grunted. "How do I get to Jason?"

"Through the front office. Through Tom Bradford." She grinned impishly at him over the olive left in her glass.

"Let's go eat," Larry said.

"Let's do."

After they were seated in the Acro dining room and Larry had ordered lunch, he asked his next question.

"Could Miss Fanny get me into Jason's office?"

"No. She doesn't speak to him or to the snippet. And he no longer goes to the office—a semi-invalid."

147

"Interesting case," Larry said. "Does Tom Bradford have any fun?"

"I'm not sure. I doubt it. He used to have a very devoted secretary, I've heard; but she quit the firm after a few years of dedicated service. I never knew her name."

"I see," Larry said.

Their lunch arrived. Larry mined Dora for further background on several of his Golden Givers, but he did not press her about Jason Hill or any of the others.

After lunch he did not return to his room, but went in person to an employment agency to arrange for permanent stenographers for campaign headquarters. The manager was a blue-haired ex-secretary who reminded him of Miss Mary, back in David Chancellor's office.

He explained his needs and then asked, "You couldn't, by any chance, spare the time to help us, could you?"

"Oh, no," she said, flattered. "I couldn't possibly leave here, even for a few days."

"You would be ideal," he said. "I need someone like you for my girl Friday, an executive secretary who knows all the really important people in town. After all, this is a fund-raising campaign."

He spoke as though he were confiding in her, sharing a secret. She took the bait and unconsciously lowered her own voice.

"I know exactly what you mean."

"Sure you do. Do you know anyone of wide experience, say with Midwest Mills, or Schwartz and Company, or Hill Enterprises—any of the really first-class firms—who might be available? This is humanitarian work, you know."

"I know girls who have worked for all of them. There's Mildred Holt, who was with Midwest for years—but she's quite old now, arthritis and all. Then there's Hilda Schaeffer, Mr. Schwartz's own private secretary, retired. She might do it. And Nell Hargreaves. She was at Hill Enterprises for some time. Kind of snooty, but competent. I'm not sure what she's doing now. Takes care of her mother, I've heard. Of course, none of them are listed in our files."

"Well, I want to give you my business. It was just a thought. I can get along with a pair of beginners, if I have to, until our volunteers come in."

So he hired two recent business-school graduates for temporary work. Then he went back to his room and located Hilda Schaeffer, and through her Nell Hargreaves, and employed both of them full time beginning Monday morning.

20

$ $ $

LARRY SPENT FRIDAY WITH SAM ALGOOD AND THE TWO TYPISTS, junior grade, preparing stories for Sam to plant in the Sunday editions of the newspapers. The mayor's proclamation declaring November "Physical Fitness Month" was done up brown, and the names of the Mayor's Committee were ready to go. One story announced the Kickoff Banquet for the next Friday. Another told of Stanley Hogan's preliminary plans for the Fiz-Fit parade on Saturday.

Sam's before-and-after picture story of the progress of the makeshift gymnasium sponsored by the Federal Physical Fitness Foundation was prepared but reserved for the first Sunday in November, the day after the parade. Larry allowed himself to be interviewed. He had fine things to say about the

President's Physical Fitness Program and about the Federal Foundation—hinting at but never establishing a positive tie-in. He also praised the work of the Physical Fitness Council of Corinth, the Mayor of Corinth, and the wonderful people he had met and expected to meet in Corinth. From the enthusiasm already exhibited, he was certain of a highly successful campaign. Corinth was assured a first-class gymnasium for its youth, its number-one resource.

Sam brought in the invitations to the Kickoff Banquet and had firm dates for the delivery of the rest of the campaign literature. The council members returned their organization charts with two hundred and forty key personnel to man the various committees. Almost as many Call Girls had been recruited.

Charlie Shanks came in on Saturday morning with two dozen volunteer typists on loan, and promises of as many more. He had also lined up a number of Wind Bags to take the word to the city's numerous service clubs.

Things were well in hand when the Old Guard gathered at Angelo's for Saturday-night supper.

"You dear friends will have to feed me all next week," Sam said after they had ordered. "I went off salary as of five o'clock this afternoon."

"Why, Sam?" Pat asked in alarm. "What happened?" She looked at Larry to see if he showed signs of anger.

"I bet this unprincipled Simon Legree of ours my next week's paycheck that he'd never get Big Jack Hopkins to head the Campaign Committee."

"You didn't really," Pat said accusingly. "You didn't bet against us."

"I sure did, but he'll never make a sucker out of me again."

"You and your penny-ante bets," Larry said. "You couldn't get another bet with me. I'm out of your class now. I'm taking ten-thousand-dollar wagers."

"Ten thousand?" Scotty's eyes popped.

"With whom?" Sam asked.

"Dora."

"Dora?" Pat's eyes did something.

"On what?" Sam asked.

"It's a secret until the pay-off. Just like ours, Sam."

"Dora's good at keeping secrets," Sam said slyly. "And shrewd. You might lose that one."

"She thinks she has a cinch. And she may have. Anyway, she's covered."

Sam's raised eyebrow was for Larry alone.

Momma's steaks made polite conversation difficult for the next half hour. After the steaks, torpor set in.

Larry was satisfied with the Sunday newspapers. He loafed all morning but dressed for lunch and spent the afternoon directing the porters as they moved tables and chairs into the mezzanine ballroom, which was to serve as Campaign Headquarters. By bedtime, telephones had been installed, typewriters and adding machines brought in, and standards placed by the tables for signs designating the categories of workers.

The permanent secretaries, Hilda Schaeffer and Nell Hargreaves, reported for work promptly at nine Monday morning. Hilda was a square frau past retirement age, but neat and efficient looking, perhaps a little domineering. Larry set her to work cutting stencils for the Confidential Messages to be handed out at the banquet.

Nell Hargreaves was something else. Not yet forty, she had the rigorously disciplined figure and immaculate grooming of the top-flight confidential secretary. She was the one all right—Tom Bradford's ex-mistress.

"And now, what's my job, Mr. Shelton?" she asked with a half-amused smile.

"I want you to direct my Call Girls when they start coming in," he said, watching her face.

"Call Girls?" No expression at all.

"Telephone corps," he said. "Come with me to the executive desk. I have several lists, with the messages for each."

151

He escorted her to his desk and showed her to a stenographer's chair halfway behind it. He sat down in his own chair and picked up a list of names—his make-believe poker hand for the highest stakes in the game.

"Let's see, Miss Hargreaves. You were Tom Bradford's secretary, I believe."

"Yes."

"Consider yourself my confidential secretary. If you don't like the job, you can demote yourself."

No expression.

"I am a fund raiser, a professional. Certain procedures are necessary in my work, routine—magic, miracles, pulling rabbits out of hats. I must have a hundred-thousand-dollar donor to impress my co-workers at the banquet on Friday of this week, four days from now. I have the donor picked—Jason Hill."

An expression at last—pity for an idiot.

"You are my avenue of approach."

"Me?" She showed some surprise.

"Yes. Through Tom Bradford."

"I believe you are mistaken, Mr. Shelton." Nell Hargreaves sounded exactly the way she looked. "I no longer work for Hill Enterprises. I have lost all contact with the firm and with Mr. Bradford."

"I know that."

"Yet you think I could get Mr. Bradford to arrange it so you could solicit Mr. Hill?"

"Yes. I believe one telephone call from you would open the door."

"Do you have reason to believe that?"

"Yes, an excellent reason."

"How long have you been in Corinth?"

"One week and one day."

"And you found me and hired me and have the audacity to ask such a favor of me?" The expression was no longer one of pity for an idiot.

152

"Yes. I am a conscienceless money hunter."

"Magic did you say? Miracles?" She smiled at last, but not happily. "I suppose I would be wasting time if I asked who told you."

"No one told me. On my honor, such as it is, the only person I have talked to that even knew your name was the Mrs. Reynolds who operates an employment agency; and I doubt that she ever saw you or knows exactly what your position was."

"So do I. I've merely talked to her on the telephone—about job applications at Hill."

"That's it, Miss Hargreaves. All of it." He spread his hands as if to show his cards. "You may demote yourself if you like."

"Do you really think you could separate a hundred thousand dollars from Jason Hill's estate?"

Larry noted that she did not say from Jason Hill. He noted, too, the tempered steel in her gray eyes.

"I make my living this way, Miss Hargreaves. This is my profession."

"No one has ever got a nickel of that money."

"Not yet." Larry smiled.

"If I thought you could—"

"I can," Larry assured her.

Slowly, deliberately, Nell Hargreaves reached for the telephone.

"Is this an outside line?" she asked.

"Yes, they all are—special cable."

Without hesitation she dialed a number from memory.

"Mr. Bradford," she said, and waited for a few seconds.

"Tom? This is Nell. . . . Yes . . . fine. How are you?

"I've just met a most remarkable man. I never saw him before in my life. He wants to talk to Jason Hill. He wants you to arrange it."

She sat and listened, poker-faced, for several seconds more.

"Tom, *I* want you to arrange it. I think it might be the

153

wisest thing you ever did. . . . No, I told you I never saw him before in my life. . . . His name is Shelton. He's a professional, of some standing in his field, I believe." She smiled again, grimly.

"He has four days. . . . Of course he's serious. So am I —No, don't call me. Just arrange it. . . . That would leave him three days. . . . Indeed, I do advise it."

She put the telephone down.

"Mr. Bradford has to take some papers out to the Hill place tomorrow afternoon for Jason's signature. He'll arrange for you to go with him. Be in his office at two thirty."

"Thank you, Miss Hargreaves," Larry said.

"Don't thank me, Mr. Shelton. Just pry a hundred thousand dollars out of that estate, and we'll call it even. Now, I'll demote myself to acting as madam of your Call Girls." Her smile was real this time.

Larry took out his cardcase and handed Nell Hargreaves one of his business cards.

"Whenever you want a job as my confidential secretary for real, just report to that address," he said.

She put the card into her purse, but she was already reading the message clipped to the first list of clients for the Call Girls.

Campaign Headquarters rapidly came alive. By ten o'clock the telephone corps had twenty lines busy at the same time. Pat came in late, breathless—she had had to go in her own car to get the vocational nurse for the morning session. Other council members coming in and out soon learned to look to her as much as to Larry for instructions. She was taking over like an old pro. Larry looked forward to the day when she would be his number-one Associate.

Larry went over his check sheet. Everything was working. From his calendar he made individual schedules for briefing the various committee chairmen, their committees, and then their entire corps of workers. He took half an hour with Stanley Hogan, going over the parade route; an hour with

154

the catering service, detailing the Kickoff Banquet; a brief, barely courteous courtesy call (telephone) to the mayor; lunch suddenly before him on his desk—Pat, naturally; several cups of coffee, unordered; and before he knew it Hilda Schaeffer was reminding him that it was closing time.

Nell Hargreaves materialized when Hilda had removed her bulk.

"The calls made are coded," she said. "Plus, minus, busy, no answer."

"How are the girls doing?"

"They're catching on fast. Do you want me to go over the completed lists with you?"

"No. You're doing fine," he said, after a glance at the first two or three pages. "Keep at this in the morning."

"Good night, then," she said.

"Good night." He looked up to see Dora Mansfield approaching his desk. He watched the two women meet and nod at each other with no apparent sign of recognition or of interest. He deliberately focused his attention on the files open on his desk.

"Busy, busy, busy," Dora said accusingly.

"Oh, hi, Dora," he said, looking up again. " 'Bastard, bastard, bastard,' my sister always says."

"She ought to know." Dora sat down in the stenographer's chair. "Can I help?"

"In that?" he asked. She was wearing a chinchilla stole over a dinner dress. She looked like a million of her dollars.

"I can't very well get out of it here in the ballroom. I'd rather you put those papers away and let me buy you a drink before I join a party for dinner."

"Go ahead," Larry said, closing the last file and planting a paperweight on the stack. "Corrupt me."

"I intend to."

They rose, and he let her guide him out of the ballroom and into a small bar on the mezzanine.

"Martini?" she asked while the waiter was showing them to a table.

"Scotch and soda tonight," he said, holding her chair.

She gave the order.

"It's good to be a gigolo again," he said when he was seated facing her.

"Again?"

"I'm always preying on unsuspecting women."

"But I'm a suspecting woman. What gives with Pat?"

"Pat? Oh, yes, the little girl from the laundry."

"Yes, the little girl from the laundry." Dora mimicked his speech.

"I don't know. What gives? She seems like a nice kid."

"She's nice to *you*. She brought your lunch to you. And she left orders for coffee to be brought to you at intervals even after she had gone back to her washtub. Or didn't you notice?"

"I don't suppose I did. I must remember to thank her."

"Indeed, you must." Dora signed the bar bill which came with their drinks. "That's the very least you can do."

They tasted their drinks, then sipped in earnest. "Pat told us she knew you," Dora continued. "That she had worked on a previous campaign with you."

"Yes, a church. A good campaigner as I remember."

"And I'll bet you remember. So does she. Really, Larry, busy as she is, she sort of manages to hover over you."

"A born social worker. But then I bring out the mother in women." He gave Dora his Miss Mary smile.

"Don't try that on me. I'm the least maternal woman you'll ever meet. Forget it. I'm just clearing the air. Want to pump me some more?"

"Fifty-thousand-dollar class?"

"There's no such class," Dora told him. "But you're getting closer. How are you coming along with your golden dream—the hundred-G mirage?"

"Just waiting for a signature on the check."

"Show me that and I'll believe in your second bracket."

But she did give him a rundown on some people who were able, if militantly unwilling, to part with fifty G's. And she gave him more—sprightly companionship and subtle feminine encouragement, nothing motherly about it.

When she left him, he felt the old excitement rising. Even without Sam's preview he would have pegged her the minute she entered his suite the night of the first council meeting. He had met her before, in a dozen campaigns. He smiled with satisfaction as he rode the elevator up to his room. As long as he retained that touch, luck was with him, and professional pride. As long as he could size up women, and men, and calculate what, how much, and when they would give, he was still in business.

21

$ $ $

TUESDAY MORNING WAS LIKE MONDAY MORNING, BUT SOME-what better organized. Hilda had the help of four volunteer typists. Nell's Call Girls had lost their amateur standing. Their calls were yielding more and more plusses. Larry had his desk cleared and was able to spend much of his time on the floor. Frequently he found Pat at his elbow, helping or learning how to help more efficiently.

She was at his elbow when Dora dropped in for a stint at

the Golden Givers table. Dora spoke and raised an eyebrow as she passed, but went directly to join the evaluating committee making a preliminary estimate of the big donors' potential. She told Larry goodbye when she left, a few minutes before twelve. Pat was gone by one thirty.

Larry put Nell Hargreaves in charge when he excused himself at two. She was the only one he would not have had to tell where he was going. He took a taxi from the hotel cabstand to the Hill Building. He handed his card to a receptionist at two twenty-five.

"I believe Mr. Bradford is just leaving," she said a trifle haughtily.

"I know. I'm going with him," Larry said, for its shock value.

The girl was still in mild shock when she ushered him into Tom Bradford's office.

Tom Bradford was an offensively athletic bronze Olympian with graying temples. He offered no hand to his visitor.

"You're wasting your time and mine, Shelton," he said gruffly.

"You know my business?"

"I read your card and I've seen your name in the paper. You'll never get a nickel out of Jason Hill."

"I mean, you know my business better than I do?" Larry saw no point in trying to be friendly.

"In this instance, yes," Bradford said with a crooked, humorless smile. "As you seem to know mine, if I'm to believe what I hear over the telephone."

"I'd believe it if I were you, Bradford." Larry did not bother to smile. He followed Tom Bradford into a private elevator, without invitation, and rode down twenty-eight silent stories into the basement garage.

Bradford's car was waiting. Tom drove himself. The loudest noise inside the car during the fifteen-mile drive out to Hillside was the ticking of the clock. They drove through the gate in an iron fence, along a half mile of landscaped drive-

158

way, up to the ivy-covered façade of a Tudor country house. Tom pulled up behind a Thunderbird and stopped.

Assuming that was the place, Larry got out of the car and preceded Tom Bradford to the door. He even rang the bell, but when it was opened by a smiling young patrician who would never have been mistaken for a maid, he stepped aside.

"Hi, Tom," the woman said brightly.

"Hi, Sandra. Mrs. Hill, this is Mr. Shelton. He wants to talk to Jason."

So the snippet was named Sandra.

"Hello, Mr. Shelton. Come in." She was graciousness itself. Obviously she had not been forewarned. "Jason is in the solarium, by the pool."

She led the way. It was a joy to follow her—just far enough behind for a good view of a grade-A snippet in motion. All this, and millions too, Larry thought. No wonder Tom Bradford was loath to lead a poacher into his domain.

"How is Jason today?" Bradford asked.

"Fine. He's soaking up this autumn sunshine like a lazy old tomcat."

Larry questioned the validity of her simile.

The solarium had undoubtedly been built as a conservatory, but the planters had been replaced by a long, narrow swimming pool. A tiled walk ran all the way around the pool. The old tomcat sat in a chromium-tubing beach chair on the west walk, bathed by the slanting rays of the midafternoon sun.

Jason Hill's body was thin, but hardly frail. His face was thin, too, accentuated by a bushy white mane and bushy eyebrows.

"Jason, this is Mr. Shelton. Tom brought him to see you." Sandra seemed to accept Larry, since Tom had brought him.

"Mr. Shelton." The old man's voice was firm, and so was the hand he extended.

"Mr. Hill," Larry said. He was glad it had been the snippet who introduced him.

Jason exchanged greetings with Tom Bradford and asked a few routine questions about Hill Enterprises.

"Tom, why don't you and I take a swim while Jason and Mr. Shelton have their chat?" Sandra suggested.

"Will we have time?" Tom looked at Jason.

"Of course we will," the snippet said. "You'll be staying for dinner—and Mr. Shelton, too, if we can prevail upon him."

No one argued with Sandra; so she and Tom went off to change, and Larry pulled up a chair and sat beside Jason Hill.

"I know your business, Mr. Shelton," Jason said when they were alone.

"Yes. I'm sure Mr. Bradford told you."

"No. Tom didn't even tell me he was bringing you out, but I read the papers. In fact, it's not at all like Tom to bring you. That's why I'm going to listen—for a few minutes, at least—to find out why he did."

"I'm sure he's a public-spirited citizen—as his position with Hill Enterprises would indicate—and he's interested in the youth of Corinth."

"Not Tom," the old man said positively. "I trained him. He doesn't care a damn about the youth of Corinth, and neither do I."

"Do you have any grandchildren, Mr. Hill?"

"No. No children either."

"But I thought perhaps, Mrs. Hill, your daughter-in-law—"

"Sandra is my wife." Jason turned to look directly into Larry's face, which Larry tried to keep as impassive as possible.

"I'm sorry," Larry said.

"Well, I'm not. I'm quite happy about it."

"As you rightly should be."

How true his statement was Larry fully realized when Tom and Sandra came out of their dressing rooms and plunged into the pool. Sandra was some snippet. Larry could understand Miss Fanny's—any plain woman's—innate aversion to her. She had everything, in just the right proportions.

160

"You people are crazy," Jason said abruptly. "Asking me or anybody else to provide playthings for kids whose own parents haven't earned them."

"It's not the kids' fault," Larry countered.

"It's not mine, either. That's the trouble with this country today. Too many people getting something they never earned. All I pay for is work or ideas."

Sandra and Tom emerged at the other end of the pool and walked toward a low diving board. A perceptive female might have had some complimentary things to say about Tom's physique.

"A handsome pair," Larry observed.

Old Jason nodded.

"Do you swim much, sir?" Larry asked.

"Every day. Therapy. Does me good."

"Too bad you don't have a flock of kids around here. They'd enjoy this pool. You might enjoy them, too."

"I've never missed them."

Larry and Jason Hill both silently watched the swimmers dive off the low board.

"Used to swim in the river when I was a boy," the old man said. "Where'd you swim?"

"Everywhere. Anywhere. I guess I enjoyed swimming most when I used to visit my Uncle Joe down in Texas."

"Texas, huh?" Jason seemed willing to keep the conversation clear of fund raising.

"Yes. Uncle Joe had quite a spread down there, the Double J, thousands of acres. I guess I enjoyed swimming in the stock tank about a quarter of a mile from his house better than anywhere else in the world."

"Never been to Texas," Jason said. "Always wanted to go."

"I spent several summers there. Uncle Joe was Dad's oldest brother. He didn't have any children of his own; so he sort of took to me. Spoiled me, I guess. He and Aunt Belle both. When I was in my teens I thought she was the most

161

beautiful woman in the world. She wasn't over eight or ten years older than I was. And I guess she *was* a beauty."

Tom and Sandra were resting then, sitting on the side of the pool, talking and occasionally looking toward Jason and Larry. She probably knew Larry's business by that time. He wondered if his invitation to dinner still stood.

"Then there was Bret, Uncle Joe's top hand," Larry rambled on. "Uncle Joe was sort of laid up. Bret ran the place. He used to go swimming with me and Aunt Belle, and let us ride the range with him. I thought he was wonderful, too. I suppose kids have a capacity for wonder. Too bad we lose it when we grow older."

Larry stretched out in his chair, and yawned. The divers were at it again.

"This sun sure feels good," he said.

"I guess you're a wealthy man yourself, Mr. Shelton," Jason said.

"No. Just an average guy trying to get along." Larry spoke lazily.

"But your Uncle Joe. I would assume that you were his heir."

"No," Larry drawled. "No. Funny thing about that. Uncle Joe kicked off suddenly with a heart attack while I was still in high school. Aunt Belle got everything—ranch, oil— everything. She married Bret, and they had a house full of kids. They're all doing well. My rich relatives—no blood kin, of course."

Larry chuckled at the irony of it all.

Jason Hill had no further comment, and Larry merely yawned again. Seeing the lull in the conversation, Tom and Sandra swam over in front of them and climbed out of the pool. Tom helped Sandra to her feet.

"Have you two finished your chat?" she asked, no less brightly than she had spoken earlier.

"I think so." Larry rose.

"Not entirely," Old Jason said, studying, not Larry, but

his top hand and his snippet. "How much did you say you had me down for, Mr. Shelton?"

"Our evaluating committee tentatively set the sum at two hundred thousand dollars," Larry said evenly.

"Ridiculous!" the old man exploded. "I won't give you a penny more than a hundred thousand. Tom, you have a checkbook in that brief case, haven't you?"

"Er—er—ah, yes, Jason." Tom was on the verge of exploding too.

"Well, get it and make out a check for a hundred thousand dollars to—" Jason looked up at Larry expectantly.

"Federal Physical Fitness Foundation," Larry said. "Put Corinth Fund down in the corner."

"Now?" Tom asked, still immobilized by shock.

"Now!" Jason barked.

Tom came alive and opened his dispatch case posthaste. He remembered to dry his hands and chest before producing the folio-size checkbook and opening it. He fumbled in the case for a fountain pen, which he ultimately found.

Larry glanced at Sandra when Tom began writing the check. She was smiling at him enigmatically—La Gioconda Snippetina. She might really adore the old tomcat after all.

After Tom Bradford had written the check and signed it, he handed the folio to Jason for him to countersign. Then he risked looking at Larry. Pure distilled essence of venom, two hundred proof. Larry tried to return the crooked, humorless smile he had received from Bradford when they first met. He could not keep it humorless.

"Here you are, Mr. Shelton." The perforated lines popped as Jason Hill tore the check out of the folder to hand to Larry. "Tell that evaluating committee of yours that they are as crazy as hell. Putting me down for two hundred thousand dollars! Preposterous!"

"I'll relay the message, sir," Larry said. "And may I thank you on behalf of the foundation and all the kids in Corinth?"

"You may not. Thank me on your own behalf. I know what the customary fee is for you fund raisers."

"Well, sir, I thank you personally on my own behalf."

"You're welcome." The old man sounded sincere.

"Will you stay for dinner, Mr. Shelton?" Sandra would still prevail upon him.

"No, Mrs. Hill, I really can't. I have desk work piled a mile high back in town."

"Too bad. Tom's staying. I'll send you back into town in one of our own cars." She drew a robe on and went to call the garage.

Tom stood around like a bronze statue while Larry and Jason Hill chatted about nothing. Presently Sandra appeared in the solarium door, and beckoned. "This way, Mr. Shelton."

Before Larry reached her, he heard Jason call to him.

"By the way, Mr. Shelton, have you ever been to Texas?"

Larry turned for a moment. He could not see, but he would have sworn that the old man's eyes were twinkling.

"No, sir," he said. "I never have. Always wanted to go."

Jason Hill might have been solicited; but, by God, he had not been conned. He had merely bought an idea—and paid.

22

$ $ $

LARRY'S DAY BEGAN EARLY, ABOUT DAYBREAK, WITH A TELE-
phone call from Tom Bradford.

"Listen, Shelton," Tom began, "I want to know exactly
what you told Jason Hill yesterday."

"I told him about the gymnasium fund drive," Larry
answered sleepily.

"I mean about me."

"As I remember, the only remark I made was that you
cut a fine figure in swim trunks."

"Do you expect me to believe that?"

"I don't give a damn what you believe."

"I believe you told him some cock-and-bull story that up-
set him. Several times during the evening I caught him looking
at me with a puzzled expression on his face—watching me."

"I think you'll bear watching, Bradford," Larry said. "But
I didn't mention it to the old man. We merely discussed kids
and indulged in some reminiscences of our own boyhood." So
Jason had not figured out how Larry gained entrée to Hillside.

"Bull—"

"You seem to have cocks and bulls on your mind this
morning, Bradford," Larry interrupted. "You'd better forget

165

the livestock and concentrate on Hill Enterprises. I may be directing another campaign here sometime, and I'd like to think the firm would still be solvent."

"You—you stick your head into my business again—sometime—after—"

"After you're in full control? Watch it, Bradford. I can always appeal to Mrs. Hill, in memory of her sainted first husband."

Tom Bradford broke the connection, presumably by slamming the receiver down.

Larry grinned and then yawned, but he got out of bed and headed for a cold shower.

Nell Hargreaves met him at his desk in Campaign Headquarters, ostensibly to receive instructions for her day's work. She was much too well disciplined to ask him how he came out with Jason Hill.

"First, I'd like you to take this check over to Shawn Brothers, who are auditing the campaign for us." He handed her Jason Hill's check, face up, so she could see the amount and the signatures. "Ask them to acknowledge it and to hold it for us until Friday night. You may tell them why. Bring the receipt back to me. Would you like to do that for me, Miss Hargreaves? Personally?"

"I'd love to do that for you, Mr. Shelton. Personally," she said, with a smile of grim satisfaction.

"And no one else need know about the check until the banquet. Don't spoil our grandstand play."

"You know I wouldn't." She hesitated a moment before leaving his desk. "Mr. Shelton, I won't say I'm glad you—you found me and got me into this. But I will say that I harbor no ill will."

"Thank you," Larry said to her back as she departed for Shawn Brothers.

It was just as well that Larry had been aroused early and so had had time to clear his desk pile before Campaign Headquarters opened officially. He directed a big trailer truck full of campaign materials to Stanley Hogan and Scotty Mac-Gregor to be unloaded at the old laundry. He gave Stan invoices for things to be used in the parade, and instructed Scotty as to how he wanted other materials stored in the gymnasium so they would be readily available when needed.

The rest of Wednesday and most of Thursday were devoted to minute details of the banquet and the parade. By closing time Thursday, Larry's various check lists were complete. Only Hilda Schaeffer, Nell Hargreaves, and a skeleton crew of Call Girls reported Friday morning to answer telephone inquiries and to make such last-minute changes as might be necessary.

Larry himself knocked off Friday afternoon when the hotel crew came in to set up the ballroom for the Kickoff Banquet.

"Leave the telephones, typewriters, and adding machines on the tables," he instructed the head porter. "Add tables where needed, but keep the standards and signs as they are. Make the place as attractive as you can, but leave it looking busy—as much like a workshop as a banquet hall."

Only Hilda and Nell stayed on to answer telephones. After a late lunch Larry lay down and slept until six o'clock.

He looked in on the arrangements at seven, stood on the speaker's rostrum for a good view, approved what he saw, and retired to the little bar off the mezzanine for a Scotch and soda before the guests arrived. When the mezzanine began to hum, he left the bar and stood around unobtrusively watching the Key Personnel exchange their invitations for sealed envelopes marked

CONFIDENTIAL
Do not open until told to do so.

The Physical Fitness Council of Corinth was on hand to act as hosts, and a crew of attractive usherettes recruited from the corps of Gold Diggers showed the guests to their seats.

167

After the rank and file of Key Personnel had been placed, Larry slipped in among the council members to be seated, along with the Mayor's Committee, at the head table, which stretched all the way across one end of the ballroom.

Stanley Hogan served as master of ceremonies, a role he fitted far better than that of petitioner. After the invocation by an Episcopalian rector, dinner was served, to organ music provided by a musically inept but financially loaded debutante.

During dessert, Stan rose to introduce the head table and distinguished guests, the names rolling off his tongue deliciously. The mayor extended his greetings, and Stan introduced Dr. Rankin, a keynoter who loved his work. Then Charlie Shanks had the honor of introducing Larry, "—one of the country's most outstanding consultants on community funds."

"Thank you, Charlie," Larry said, as he came to the microphone. "Mr. Mayor, members of the council and of the Mayor's Committee, distinguished guests, ladies and gentlemen. And you, too, Stan."

An appreciative chuckle went around the various tables.

"Stan omitted one distinguished guest—an invited guest—who, however, is unable to be with us tonight.

"I refer to the First Donor, that distinguished person in every campaign like this who has the honor of making the first gift to a worthy cause such as ours.

"I am going to ask Mr. Shawn—of Shawn Brothers, who are auditing this campaign—to read the distinguished First Donor's message to this assembly. Mr. Robert Shawn—"

Larry stepped aside to make room at the microphone for one of the Shawn brothers.

"Ladies and gentlemen," Robert Shawn began rather unimpressively, "I have here a check for one hundred thousand dollars signed by Jason Hill."

He waved the check over his head to a momentarily quiet, thoroughly stunned audience of three hundred and sixty Corinthians. Then a little hand clapping—begun by Dora Mans-

168

field, Larry thought—grew into a mighty roar of applause, during which the Shawn brother solemnly repocketed the check and sat down again.

Larry was clapping his hands when he returned to the microphone.

"I join you," he began, as soon as he could be heard, "in your resounding ovation to Mr. Jason Hill, our esteemed First Donor. I only wish he were here to witness this show of appreciation.

"With such a beginning, we cannot but finish gloriously. However, I must remind you that not every gift will be as easily come by as this munificent gesture on the part of Mr. Hill." He thought he heard another chuckle start around the tables; but he hurried to cut it off, gratifying though it was —a vindication of Charlie's glowing introduction of Larry as "one of the country's most outstanding consultants on community funds."

"We have a busy month ahead of us," he continued earnestly, and then went into his pitch.

He had gained the respect—and the rapt attention—of the Key Personnel, whom he proceeded to instruct in the fine art of money hunting.

"Detailed suggestions on the part each one of you will play in the campaign are in the sealed envelopes addressed to you individually and marked confidential.

"All right. Hold the envelope in your left hand—thus."

He held a sealed envelope up before him.

"Grasp the upper-right-hand corner of the envelope between the thumb and forefinger of your right hand—thus.

"At the sound of the C-major chord by the lovely Miss Lynda Wheeler, let her rip!"

At his signal, the lovely Miss Lynda Wheeler blasted out a full-volume, full-organ C-major chord—true for once— which drowned out the ripping of three hundred and sixty confidential envelopes. In the relative quiet which followed, Larry got in his final instructions.

169

"Take your confidential messages home with you. Mull them over during the week end and man your stations Monday morning. Remember the parade tomorrow at ten.

"Good night, all."

Larry knew that Miss Fanny was spry, but he had never realized how spry until he saw her sprinting toward him and the Shawn brother at the end of the meeting.

"Robert—Robert, let me see that check," she demanded.

"Let me see it," she repeated, as the Shawn brother took his time about producing the bombshell.

When he handed it to her, she examined it closely through the bay windows in her bifocals.

"It's Jason's signature, all right," she admitted. "And it's for a hundred thousand dollars.

"He did it just to shame me," she said, her voice rising in indignation. "Jason Hill never gave a penny to anything before in his life. He did it to shame me, I tell you! I've never been so humiliated since I was born.

"Robert Shawn, wait right here. I'll show Jason Hill. I'll write you a bigger check than his."

Miss Fanny snatched her purse open and fished out a personal checkbook.

"I'll give you a check for a hundred and fifty—for a hundred and one thousand dollars—right here, right now."

Resting her checkbook on the speaker's lectern, she angrily wrote a check for one hundred and one thousand dollars and handed it to Robert Shawn, who carefully placed it beside Jason's check in his breastpocket wallet.

"I'll call my bank first thing in the morning and tell them to have the money available," Miss Fanny said. "That'll teach Jason Hill to suck eggs."

Dora Mansfield had sidled up to Larry's elbow during Miss Fanny's outburst.

"Looks like I've lost a bet," she said, squeezing Larry's arm.

"Taking candy from a baby," Larry said smugly.

"Candy? Come with me." She led him through the thinning crown to an elevator just outside the ballroom. The banqueters were using stairs and escalators.

"Garage," she said to the operator.

"Where are we going?" he asked, as if he did not know.

"For a drive down the river road. You've had a hard day."

"That I have," Larry agreed, choosing to ignore his long afternoon nap.

"Calls for an easy night," Dora said as the elevator came to a stop in the basement garage.

The attendant recognized Dora and whisked her white Continental up before them in a matter of seconds.

"Thank you, George," she said.

Larry tipped the attendant, who held the door for Dora to slide in under the wheel.

"How did you do it?" she asked, after she had pulled out into traffic. "Or is it a trade secret?"

"It's a trade secret."

"Not revealed in any of those confidential messages, either, I'll bet."

"No."

"Maybe I won't bet, after all. I should learn." She maneuvered the car expertly in and out of the downtown traffic and onto a freeway along the riverbank. A few miles out of town she left the freeway, crossed a bridge, and turned onto a winding road along the opposite bank. Soon the road angled away from the river, leaving a strip of landscaped summer places with boathouses backed up to the water.

Dora turned into one of the driveways.

"Would you be interested in a drink or two, Mr. Shelton?" she asked.

"I'd be interested in whatever might be hidden away in one of these retreats," Larry said.

"I thought you would be." Dora chuckled throatily.

The automobile lights lit up a low-roofed stone-and-glass

cottage nestling in weeping willows. Dora turned ninety degrees, and stopped.

"This is down the river road, as I said." She chuckled again as she switched off the engine and lights.

Larry went around to her side to help her out of the car. She barely brushed against him as she accepted his assistance.

"Come in, fly," she said at the door of the cottage. "Fly-by-night, that is."

When she turned on the lights, the cottage proved to be quite luxuriously furnished, and as feminine as Dora herself.

"The makings are over here," she said, leading the way to the bar in a far corner of the room.

"Brandy, maybe?" she asked.

"Brandy, certainly."

Dora slid behind the bar, where she produced two inhalers and a bottle of Armagnac 1924.

"Pour," she said. She came around the end of the bar, sat down on a high stool beside Larry, and piled her stole on another.

Larry splashed brandy into the snifters and slid one over in front of her. She cupped both hands around the bulge in the glass and looked at their reflections in the bar mirror.

"A handsome couple, don't you think?" she asked.

"Charming." Larry raised his glass, sniffed appreciatively, and dribbled some of the brandy onto his tongue.

Dora did the same. Neither said anything for a while.

"Now that we've admired ourselves, we can find more comfortable seats than these," she said, easing off the bar stool.

"Fetch." She indicated the bottle, which Larry picked up before following her over to a low divan. He put the bottle on a cocktail table and sat down beside her again.

"My hands are not doing much for this brandy," she said. "They're too cold." She slipped her right hand into his left. It was cool.

"You're good, Larry," she said, as her hand began warming up. "I like a man who's good. I don't care whether he's a good golfer, a good saxophone player, or a good preacher—just so he's good."

What was it Sam had written about Dora? *Last year it was progressive jazz; the year before, theosophy.*

"Do you understand what I'm saying, Larry? I'm saying I like you." She turned her face up to be kissed.

Larry obliged. Dora was of more recent vintage than the Armagnac; but she taster better, and she was headier. They put their glasses down sometime during the introduction. Before they were much better acquainted, Dora eased him away and said, "We can be even more comfortable than this. Help me up."

Larry rose and lifted her to her feet. She paused for a standing introduction before leading him into an adjoining bedroom and turning on a night light. "See what you can find in there." She indicated a dressing room. "I had a husband once, you know," she added, in case an explanation was needed.

A light came on in the dressing room when Larry opened the door. He found several pairs of pajamas and two or three robes. He decided against pajamas.

He made a wise choice. When he went back into the bedroom, Dora was just entering from the other side. She too had chosen a robe—woven from cobwebs it seemed, as she approached Larry and stood for an affectionate reunion.

It was an easy night, just what he needed after a long hard day at the office. They did get *some* sleep. Dora proved beyond any doubt how much she liked a good man, but she was an old campaigner who knew how to send a good man away as good as he came—good for another hard day at the office.

She delivered Larry to the Acro garage in time for a shave before breakfast.

"I'll still pay my bet in coin of the realm," she reassured him, when she let him out.

"Make the check out to the foundation."

"I knew what you meant, Larry." She eased her car toward the far exit of the basement garage. Larry watched the car up the ramp. He smiled. He had not lost his touch. He was still in business.

23

$ $ $

STANLEY HOGAN WAS THE PARADE MARSHAL. HE BUZZED IN and out along the route in an Italian sports car that was almost as maneuverable as a quarter horse.

A prize-winning high-school band led off, followed by the Gold Diggers—several hundred girls in their various drill uniforms but wearing golden miners' helmets and carrying papier-mâché picks on their shoulders. The Federals, Little League Champions, played miniature baseball on a stylized diamond aboard a huge flat-bed truck. Behind them came the All-Stars appropriately suited out in the uniforms of their respective sports.

Pat Hayden, in a woolen leotard, worked with a corps of her young gymnasts and tumblers on another float. After the second band and an outdoor office staffed by smart White Collar Girls came Scotty's float—basketball practice in a large rolling cage.

Mr. Fiz Fit himself, a helium-filled muscleman, Larry's special order to the balloon makers, towered two stories high in the middle of the procession. Symbolically, a load of Wind Bags followed, speaking simultaneously from a dozen lecterns, like the voice of Babel. More floats, more bands, more drill teams, fraternal orders, ROTC, veterans' groups, high-school athletic teams, Misses This and That, clowns, a galleon overflowing with six-foot doubloons. Stan had done himself proud. Physical Fitness Month was off to a good start.

Larry watched it all from a balcony opening off the mezzanine of the Acro-Corinthus. Main Street was lined with spectators as far as he could see in either direction. At least the demos of Corinth knew that he was in town.

The parade was over by noon. Pat called after lunch.

"Where have you been, Larry?" she asked. "I tried to get you last night to tell you how happy I was about Mr. Hill's Big Gift."

"Miss Fanny's, too," Larry said, leaving her question unanswered. "She matched her cousin's donation."

"Wonderful! Two hundred thousand, and we haven't really started the campaign yet!"

"Amazing, isn't it?" Larry chuckled. It was hard to believe she still did not realize that the campaign had been under way for a full year.

"Would you like to go for a little drive out into the country?" she asked. "You must be worn out." It was she who had been tumbling all morning, not he.

"I'd like it," Larry said.

"O.K. Pick you up in half an hour?"

"Sure. I'll be out front."

She stopped in front of the Acro right on the dot, and Larry got into her car beside her.

"How about a drive down the river road?"

"Fine." Larry enjoyed drives down the river road.

Pat, as fresh and crisp as the autumn air, was in no hurry. She followed the freeway Dora had taken the night before, but much more casually.

"Were you satisfied with the parade?" she asked.

"Completely."

"I do hope the campaign goes as well—for the kids' sake and for Sam's and Red's."

"How about my sake?"

"And yours." She flashed him a smile. "But you're so strong, so confident, so self-sufficient. Do you know about Sam and Red?"

"Not as much as you know."

"Did you know that Sam's wife and two children were killed at the Indianapolis races when that car crashed into the stands? You remember."

"I remember, but I didn't know about Sam's family."

"Well, he never got over it—not until he started working with us—for you. He's been to the gym almost every day. You've seen how the kids love him."

"Yes."

"And how he loves them. And he's been a great help. He dropped out of medical school, you know."

"No. I didn't."

"He got married early and quit and went to work on a newspaper—where he always belonged, he says—but he's so good at first aid and working with injuries that I'm sure he would have made a fine doctor."

"Undoubtedly."

"Anyway, he was doing all right, had a nice home and everything. He was covering the automobile races for his paper. He took his family with him and—well—it happened. He saw it, through binoculars, from the press box. He went to pieces. He's just now picking them up. He'll make it, too, if this thing succeeds.

"But he can't take failure yet, defeat—like when the Federals lost those two games early in the season. He and Red —we had to—"

"Scotty told me about it," Larry said.

"Red's the same. He was on the road so much when he played in the big leagues that his wife—well, she did something—left him for a plumber. They had three children. She kept them. Red is good. He let *her* divorce *him.*

"But it tore him up, ruined him. His work with the Federals was just what he needed. The association did as much for him as it did for the team. They idolize him—all the kids do—and it's good for him."

Pat pulled off into a roadside park, a lookout point on a bluff affording a broad view of a bend in the river. The trees on the opposite bank made blobs of color almost dazzling in their brilliance.

"Why all this pep talk?" Larry asked. "I intend to conduct a vigorous campaign."

"I wanted you to know how much it means to so many people—what is at stake."

"I know what the stakes are," Larry reminded her. "I put them up."

"You keep telling me that, but somehow you're too defiant about it. You're afraid someone will catch you doing good. You've done a lot of good already, Larry. I know it. Scotty knows it. Red and Sam know it. Admit it."

"I haven't made a nickel out of this caper yet." Larry refused to let her inject a shot of sanctimoniousness into his blood stream.

"So you persist in the belief that you're interested only in money. Can't you be interested in people, too? The interests aren't entirely incompatible, you know." Pat kept her eyes on the view below.

"I'm interested in people. You, for instance."

"I know that. Sometimes I'm tempted to believe that you are doing all this for me—to give me a fresh start, because—"

"I can't let you believe that," Larry said quickly. By God, she was tempting as well as tempted; but by his own ground rules he had to head her off.

"There you go," she said. "You've done as much for me as you have for Red or Sam—or Scotty. You picked him up, too—remember? We've talked about it. If you're so completely dedicated to the almighty dollar, why do you go around collecting human derelicts and polishing them up?"

"Human derelicts?" he exploded, as she turned to face him. "You and Scotty, human derelicts? Young, healthy, energetic, ideal for the jobs I set up for you—"

"Yes," she said. "Young, healthy, and—discredited. He was a stevedore, and I was—I don't know exactly what I would have done. I was so ashamed, so hesitant about applying for a job in youth work, which is what I know and love. Of course, I could have hired out as a stenographer or nurse or something, but—why *did* you choose me—all of us, Larry?" Her eyes searched his face intolerably. She was ripe for kissing.

"Because I could get you cheap," he blurted out, half in self-defense.

"Cheap?" Pat's face flamed as she hastily averted it to stare at the dashboard of her car.

"If you had meant that you would never have said it, Larry," she said softly a moment later. "I don't understand you, but I know you well enough to know that you would never deliberately hurt me or Scotty or Sam or Red—or anybody."

"How do you know?"

"At the very worst, you're too smooth an operator to hurt people needlessly. You couldn't raise money the way you do if you went around offending people. You'd have to hate them. You don't hate me, do you, Larry?" She faced him suddenly, startled.

"Hate you? My God, no. Of all the people in the world—"

"You might," she went on seriously, searching his face again. "I hadn't thought of that."

"Well, don't. I'm sorry I said it, Pat. Of course I didn't mean it. I—"

"You almost got caught doing good." She was actually smiling again. "You can't stand that, can you, Larry?"

178

He merely shrugged. What could he say? What could he do? As usual, Pat baffled him, bewildered him. He could not take her on his knee like a tiny tot and explain to her in words of one syllable that she had to see him as he was, as a professional money hunter who was as dedicated to fund raising as she was to youth work—pure money hunting for its own sake, untouched by sentiment, undiluted by piety or good will, unrelated to any humanitarian purpose or human motive other than profit in a free-enterprise system.

He could not tick off his points on his fingers to convince her that supermarkets were not primarily interested in feeding a hungry populace, that airlines were not dedicated only to getting passengers from here to there, nor life-insurance companies to seeing that survivors of the deceased were secure and comfortable in their old age. Yet that was exactly where she had to start with him, with the realization that he was a businessman chasing a percentage, not Sir Galahad seeking the Grail. Those were the ground rules, *his* ground rules, of which Pat refused to become aware. That was the trouble with Pat; she was not aware. She believed TV commercials.

He was back in Suite 312 watching TV coverage of the Fiz Fit parade when Dora Mansfield called him.

"Where on earth have you been?" she asked—the same old question. "I've been calling you all afternoon."

"I've just finished dinner," he said. "I was sitting here watching television."

"What a way to spend Saturday night. Gloating, I suppose, over Mr. Fiz Fit's triumphal entry into Corinth. It looked more like Rome to me."

"The Caesars staged their spectacles after their campaigns, as I remember."

"No one would say that you weren't more forward than the Caesars. Or I. How would you like a lazy Sunday down the river road?"

"Starting when?"

"Starting about midnight. I'm at the country club now with a table of Golden Givers, but I can pick you up after the party. I'll buzz you before I leave. O.K.?"

"O.K." Larry turned his attention back to the news. The coverage of the parade was good, the commentaries favorable.

During the evening he received calls from several members of the council and other Key Personnel. Everyone was enthusiastic.

A little before eleven the bell captain delivered Sunday newspapers to his room. They too proved gratifying. Sam's before-and-after picture story of the Federal Physical Fitness Foundation program was a masterpiece. The scrawny little waifs of a year ago tugged at your heart; in the latest pictures they looked good enough to eat.

Pictures of the Kickoff Banquet and the Fiz Fit parade were scattered throughout the paper. Jason Hill, First Donor, was suitably eulogized, and Miss Fanny was featured as runner-up. The mayor and other notables received honorable mention. Larry could not have asked more.

But more would be waiting for him downstairs at midnight. He wondered what the evening might have been like if he had not goofed with Pat at Lookout Point. She had been as pleasant as ever on the drive back into town, but he had been so thoroughly perplexed by his own behavior that he had not even suggested a family dinner at Angelo's. Instead he had offered homework as an excuse for spending the evening alone. Dora's type of homework was probably just what he needed to restore his equilibrium.

Dora buzzed him again. He dressed, stuffed a toothbrush and a razor into his coat pocket, and went downstairs to meet her.

"Hi, money hunter," she said as she unlocked the door of her Continental.

"Hi, more precious than silver and gold."

"If we could only believe such nonsense," she said as he slid in beside her. "But we're too honest—I think."

180

That was it. If he could only be honest with Pat, or she with him. He was trying to be honest, but Pat— He should be thinking of Dora. She was honest—and aware—and available.

"I believe in fifty-G givers now, Larry," Dora said. "In fact, I may have lined up a few for you. A good many people share my opinion that you're pretty good—not that they're likely to press the point as I am doing." She glanced up at him possessively.

"I share your opinion, and I'm pressing the point."

"You should raise half a million before the end of the week."

"If I don't, I'll be behind schedule," Larry said. "Ten per cent of the donors have to give eighty per cent of the money. That's the way it goes."

"Then why all the hullabaloo? Why the parade and the huge work force?"

"Beating the covert, flushing out the game. You don't really sneak up on a bird and sprinkle salt on his tail. You send pointers and setters."

"Poinsettias are my favorite flowers," Dora punned to break whatever mood they were in. It was past midnight, the beginning of a lazy Sunday down the river road.

24

$ $ $

EARLY MONDAY MORNING MR. FIZ FIT, DEFLATED TO TWENTY per cent of his normal size, was permanently installed on the marquee of the Acro-Corinthus. In such an undernourished condition he was a sorry sight—scrawny, wrinkled, barely recognizable as human. Beside him was a tall thermometer-graph rising two stories up the wall of the hotel. The mercury stood at $200,000.00. A legend in ten-foot letters read:

HELP BUILD MY MUSCLES

Larry, after supervising the installation of Mr. Fiz Fit, returned to his executive desk in Campaign Headquarters, which was rapidly filling to its full complement for the real beginning of the fund drive. Hilda, Nell, and Pat handled the floor expertly, directing the volunteer workers to their stations, and interpreting the confidential messages for those who did not fully understand them.

Dora Mansfield came directly to Larry's desk.

"I think I'll do a little hovering, at least while Pat is busy on the floor," she teased.

Before Larry could comment, a matronly cherub mate-

182

rialized before him and presented a check for ten thousand dollars.

"Hello, Dora," she said first, and then introduced herself. "I'm Sybil Jones. Aaron and I couldn't attend the banquet, but here is our donation. And I want to do my part here if I can. I'm afraid I'm not very useful."

Larry thanked her for the check as he took in her slightly plump, wrinkle-free, pink-and-white innocence.

" 'Golden Givers' my confidential message says. I picked up my envelope at the door," she went on.

"Right over there, at the table under the sign. Miss Hayden will show you. We'll decide on your specific assignment." Larry turned her over to Pat, who had appeared at once to escort her to the Golden Givers table.

"Who is she?" Larry asked of Dora, who was still hovering.

"She's Mrs. Jones of the Joneses. Expect something catty?"

"Give," Larry said.

"I'm sorry, but I can't say a thing against her. Open a vein and you'll get pure indigo. She and Aaron are *the* Joneses—"

"You mean the ones everybody would like to keep up with?"

"Old families, both. Gracious, secure, thoroughbred. They give to everything. She could give more, but there may be other drives before the year's end, and she's keeping some of her charity budget in reserve. A good word from her—though I've never heard her speak ill of anyone, not even me—is the most sought-after accolade in Corinth. See how nice I can be?" Dora ended.

"I know how nice you can be," Larry said. "And how honest. Thanks, I think I can find a useful job for her."

"Anything useful I can do?"

"Yes. I have committee briefings every morning this week, but this is also the week for the Big Gifts—early, to impress and shame the pikers. See if you can set me up some luncheon, afternoon, and cocktail appointments with Golden Givers good for fifty thousand dollars and up."

"I didn't say anything about 'and up,'" Dora reminded him.

"Invite yourself where you think you can help me."

"Gee, thanks. It's good to feel wanted. I'm afraid I'm not very useful." She mimicked Sybil Jones.

"Meow," Larry said as he gathered together his papers for a committee briefing.

On his way to the conference room, Helen Boatwright buttonholed him.

"I've just had an idea, Mr. Shelton," she said eagerly. "Why don't I and some of my friends organize a picket line to picket the people and firms that refuse to give?"

"Excellent idea," Larry agreed. "But let's hold off for a while. No one has refused to give yet. Let's trust to good will first and keep the pickets in reserve. Shall we?"

"Sometimes picket lines and demonstrations are the only way to persuade people, especially rich people," she said, somewhat crestfallen. "Sometimes we have to show our anger."

"Quite right. But let's wait until we get angry. I'll tell you when." Larry eased away as gracefully as he could and hurried on to the briefing session.

Larry's week was a round of briefing sessions: Dr. Rankin's Big Boys, Red and Scotty's All-Stars, Charlie Shanks's Wind Bags, the Roll Callers, the White Collar Girls, the Gold Diggers—all those who were to work the first and second weeks—and a series of luncheon engagements, afternoon calls, and cocktail hours with Dora's select list of Golden Givers.

Wednesday, Larry got a note from Katy:

Dear Brother Grubber (Money):
What a spread! We still get the Corinth papers. David Chancellor's lilies were never arrayed like these.

What is this First Donor gimmick? The old Anonymous Donor with reverse English?
You're doing fine. We wait with bated breath.
All the best.
Your loving sibling,

KATY

The entire Physical Fitness Council, in executive session, waited with bated breath for the Shawn Brothers' audit report on Saturday afternoon. Helen Boatwright's eyes popped as she duly recorded the figures in the minutes of the council:

Golden Givers	$450,000.00
Big Boys	60,000.00
Company Men	80,000.00
All Stars (partial)	1,427.25
White Collar Girls	2,312.10
TOTAL	$593,739.35

"Phenomenal," Dr. Rankin said when he heard the total.

"Average," Larry corrected him. "The cream is always richer, and we've skimmed much of it already. Don't be disappointed at next week's audit. We still have the hard milking and the stripping to do."

"Just a simple country boy," Dora said in derision of his metaphor.

"Sounds more like a city slicker to me," Charlie Shanks, the optimist, said jubilantly. "I predict we'll go over the top in three weeks at the outside. Larry, you're a real go-getter."

"It's time I was inflating Mr. Fiz Fit," Stanley Hogan said, rising. "Is there any further business?"

There being no further business, Stan asked for a motion to adjourn, and hurried out to watch the muscleman grow to half his normal size.

Larry made a great show of preparing a copy of the auditor's report to be mailed in to his Home Office, together

185

with a not-so-showy reply for Katy to mail back to him.

"My staff in New York will evaluate this and tell us whether or not we are on schedule," he explained.

"We couldn't possibly be behind schedule, could we?" Helen Boatwright asked timorously.

"We might be," he said. She was the one who could temper enthusiasm with anxiety if anyone could.

"Are we really on schedule?" Pat asked after the others had left the conference room.

"I think so," he assured her. "Anyway, the first week's report seems to call for a celebration at Angelo's. Is the family free?"

"Red and Scotty are working two football games with the All-Stars," she said. "I'm sure Sam will be finished with his press releases by dinnertime. We can get in touch with him."

"Shall we?" He tried to catch her eye.

"I think we should," Pat said, evading his glance. "It'll mean a lot to him."

Was she thinking of Sam? Or was she playing them close to her chest? He could not resist reevaluating her chest, since the topic had arisen.

"I'll get Sam and pick you up around seven. O.K.?" She faced him.

"O.K.," he said.

His telephone was ringing when he entered Suite 312.

"Dora," a voice said in answer to his hello. "I'm still in the hotel. I wanted to remind you that tomorrow is Sunday, but your laundress was hovering."

"I need no reminding, though I welcome it." He might as well, if Pat was going to insist on Sam.

"We could start tonight, if you're free," Dora urged.

"We're having a little family celebration at Angelo's, at seven. I'll be free later."

"Do I qualify as family? Common law and all that, you know." Dora could be insistent.

"I don't know why not." If Pat could include Sam, he could invite Dora. "Red and Scotty are hustling football crowds; Sam and Pat are my family tonight."

"Goodie. I'll make a cozy foursome. Pick you up?"

"Pat's picking us up. Meet us at Angelo's. Do you know where it is?"

"I have a directory. Do I dress?"

"For dinner, yes."

She laughed and hung up.

Angelo and Momma resented the family increase, or substitution, whether the others did or not. They probably knew Dora from her pictures in the papers. Momma stuck her head out of the kitchen once, nodded to the party, hastily drew it back into the kitchen again, and kept it there all evening. Angelo was as formal as a white tie when he took their orders.

"Two martinis," he repeated after Dora and Larry had ordered.

"Three," Sam corrected him. "I can take it now, I think," he added in answer to Pat's sudden frown of apprehension.

"You're doing O.K., BTO," Sam continued, when Angelo left the table.

"Isn't he," Pat commented. If Sam's compliment had been two-edged, hers had not, at least not obviously so.

"Aren't we all," Larry said. "The campaign is coming along nicely. Everybody is doing his job well."

More talk about the fund drive continued after the cocktails arrived, and on into dinner; but the conversation lacked its usual luster, and even Momma's steaks seemed a trifle less tender than your beloved. The affair fell short of a celebration.

The air around the table was watchful. Larry watched Pat and Dora. Dora watched Pat and Larry. Sam watched all three. Only Pat seemed intent on her food, apparently devoid of suspicion.

"I can't figure that girl out," Dora said, after she had

187

shown that the Acro was out of Pat's way to Sam's boarding-house, and landed Larry safely in her car.

"Neither can I," Larry said.

"But you're sure as hell trying," Dora said, not without a tinge of jealousy. "Sorry, I can't be of any help to you on that prospect. She's either the stupidist girl child or the craftiest little bitch I've ever encountered."

"I'm not quite willing to accept either profile," Larry said. "Not yet."

"Well, I'm glad it's still an open question. Not that I'm at all possessive, but I do have my pride. I hate to see my lover's attention wandering so early in the season."

"Mere curiosity. I grant that she presents an interesting case, as you yourself admit."

"I didn't mean to admit a damned thing." Dora gunned the motor and drove savagely down the freeway toward the river-bridge exit.

That conversation set the tone of the second lazy Sunday. Not that it was a complete loss. But Dora drank a little too much. So did Larry. She alternately needled him about Pat and exaggerated her prowess in bed to provide him a sound basis for comparison if and when the occasion arose.

"There's something fishy about those family gatherings," Dora said during a rest period about the middle of Sunday afternoon. "They seem rooted in a longer acquaintanceship than the three weeks you've been in Corinth."

"You and I have become fairly well acquainted in the same length of time," Larry reminded her. They both lay on their backs, on their sides of the bed, looking up at the ceiling.

"That's what I mean. You've known Pat before, in an-other campaign, and you're forwarder than the Caesars. What I don't understand is why you didn't take up here where you left off on the other campaign. Could it be that I've taken you away from her? I'd like to think so." She liked to think so so much that she busied herself again demonstrating exactly how she effected such alienations. She was good at it—no doubt about that.

But she was hard to convince. Not long after an expert demonstration she resumed her monologue.

"Or maybe—almost certainly—you put other considerations first. You needed me—you valued my other talents, or connections, above our love life. You and your Golden Givers! Larry Shelton, you've been using me!" She rose up on one elbow and stared into his face accusingly.

"Using you?" he repeated. "It's your campaign. You invited me here to build your gymnasium."

"Did I, now? Come to think of it, Pat Hayden sold you to us. Sam Algood practically organized the council. Scotty abetted them—and that's your little family! Oh, brother, you're good. You really are. I'm just beginning to see how good." She dropped back onto her pillow and laughed aloud, almost hysterically.

"Why did I ever get mixed up with you?" she asked. "You conniving bastard. I know what your sister meant. Why, oh why, oh why?"

"Because I'm good. You told me so yourself. You like a good man, whether he's a good golfer, a good saxophone player, or a good preacher. Those were your exact words."

"But honest good. Not underhanded, not phony good. A man who drives hard, straight down the fairway."

"I didn't know about the golfer," Larry said, needled beyond his tolerance. "Last year it was progressive jazz; the year before, theosophy. Where did the hard-driving man come in?"

"God damn you, Larry Shelton. What don't you know?" She was up on her elbow again, staring down at him. "No wonder you raise big money. Most blackmailers do. But you *are* good, and I said I didn't care."

Her hot mouth smothered whatever reply he might have made. The violence of her assault drained him completely. Even Dora seemed sated at last.

After a pot of hot coffee she delivered him back to the hotel, before sunset.

"Wait a minute," she said when she let him out in the basement garage.

She opened her purse and handed him a check for twenty thousand dollars, made out to the foundation.

"Thanks," he said.

"At fifteen per cent, your fee has been three thousand dollars," she said coldly, sober now. "Is that enough?"

"More than enough," he said—to the rear bumper of the white Continental racing toward an exit ramp.

Her use of "has been" gave him a clue to the current status of their relationship, but he pocketed the check and smiled grimly as he entered the elevator.

25

$ $ $

THE CALL GIRLS HAD SEVERAL PLATOONS OF ROLL CALLERS, Homebodies, and Christian Knights lined up for briefing when Campaign Headquarters opened on November 11. Larry took the Roll Callers first—union stewards who would put the bite on labor next payday. The Homebodies, to call on wealthy shut-ins, were scheduled for Tuesday, and the Christian Knights—ministers and ushers to conduct the Health Offering on Sunday—were to meet Wednesday morning.

Larry devoted the rest of his time to tackling knotty Golden Givers in the ten-to-fifty-thousand-dollar bracket. Regularly he assigned friends or associates to solicit that group, and stepped in to assist only when asked. As he looked through the refusals, his eye caught the name of Bruce Hopkins, with the notation: "Has a good giving record in some campaigns, but says 'no' to this one. Big contractor, mayor's brother."

He beckoned Nell Hargreaves to his desk. Dora Mansfield, his chief authority on the Golden Givers, was not hovering that morning.

"Know him, Miss Hargreaves?" he asked, handing her the card.

"By reputation, yes." She read the solicitor's note.

"Would you care to elucidate? Can you comment on the comments?"

"As you see, he's a contractor—the mayor's brother. He gets more than his share of public-works contracts. Big money, socially acceptable. His wife and daughters put on quite a show."

"What has he given to, or do you know?" Larry took the card she was returning to him.

"I don't know, but I would guess that he has given to projects which offered possibilities of personal profit somewhere along the line. Could there be a rake-off on the construction of this gymnasium?" Nell Hargreaves virtually stood at attention before his desk.

"I doubt it. The whole business will be pretty closely audited by Shawn Brothers."

"Then I would assume that Bruce Hopkins shares your doubts." The slightest trace of a smile twitched the corners of her mouth.

"Thank you, Miss Hargreaves. One more question. Who would be the most likely person to succeed in a second solicitation?"

"The mayor, his brother, I would say."

"Thank you again."

191

Larry picked up his telephone and dialed the mayor's office. After running the communications gauntlet he finally heard Big Jack's voice.

"Good morning, Your Honor. This is Larry Shelton."

"Oh, yes, Shelton. What do you want?"

"I was just going over some prospect lists here, and I ran across the name of your brother. Knowing how interested you are in our campaign, I was just wondering if you might have the time to solicit him for us."

"No. No, of course not. I thought that was understood."

"You know your committee. Could you suggest one of them who might be called on to approach him?"

"No. I'm sorry." The mayor sounded eager to get off the line; but he suddenly continued, with a new note in his voice. "Wait a minute. Why don't you contact him yourself? I'll call him and ask him to see you. If I can get an appointment, I'll have my secretary notify you. How will that be?"

"Fine, Your Honor, just fine." In addition to wanting a donation, Larry was curious to find out what had caused the mayor's change of heart.

After cradling his telephone, he laid Bruce Hopkins's card aside and went on studying the stack of refusals.

He did not have to wait long. In less than half an hour the mayor's secretary called him back and told him that he had an appointment with Bruce Hopkins at eleven o'clock if he could make it.

He could make it. Indeed, the promptness with which the interview had been arranged whetted his eagerness to see what was in the air. The mayor was not trying to be helpful. Of that he was sure.

The Hopkins Construction Company had its headquarters out on the edge of town—a spacious steel-and-glass office building, a huge warehouse, and a yard full of yellow earth-moving equipment. After Larry had paid off the taxi driver, he made a quick survey of the capital investment, including the biggest Cadillac to have come off the assembly line in the last three weeks.

He entered an outer office peopled by smart stenographers and efficient young draftsmen busy at their drawing boards. A tantalizing blonde receptionist flashed him a smile and strained at her brassiere as she rose to conduct him to the boss's office.

Bruce Hopkins, a trimmer, browner version of the mayor, was alone. He removed an outsize cigar from his mouth long enough to greet Larry and bid him sit down.

"The mayor asked me to see you," Hopkins said, as if to explain his condescension.

"Yes. Very gracious of him. I suppose he told you my business."

"Indeed he did," Hopkins admitted. "You must know that one of your henchmen has already tried to put the bite on me and I practically had him thrown out."

"I wasn't aware of the manner of his exit," Larry said, smiling. "His report did mention a refusal."

"What leads you to believe that you can do any better?" Bruce Hopkins bit down firmly on his cigar and settled back to listen to Larry's pitch.

"I'm sure there has been some misunderstanding, as the mayor must have realized. I thought I might help clear it up."

"No misunderstanding. I said no. Your boy asked me for ten thousand dollars. The unmitigated gall!"

"So that's it," Larry said jovially. "Our evaluation committee underestimated your philanthropic potential. I don't blame you. I'd have thrown the piker out, too. If I had seen this layout first, I'd have put you down for fifty thousand at least."

"By God, Shelton, you *are* a fool. Your committee didn't underestimate anything. You're underestimating me. I don't intend to give a god-damned penny to your silly gymnasium. I can't afford to give to every fly-by-night promoter who invades my privacy."

Larry registered shock. It took him several seconds to recover. Bruce Hopkins was sitting tight, taking in the whole performance.

"I can't believe it," Larry said uncertainly. "I mean it just doesn't make sense. I take you for an honest man, Mr. Hopkins. This is the most elaborate setup I've ever seen in the construction business—obviously a phenomenal success. And your new car outside. And the cars your wife and daughters drive—and the clothes they wear."

Larry coughed apologetically and explained himself, "It's part of my business to gather that sort of background material, Mr. Hopkins, as you no doubt have guessed." He laughed nervously.

Bruce Hopkins nodded. He was still an interested spectator.

"Well," Larry went on, evading Hopkins's steady gaze, "I mean, it just looks plain dishonest to me for a man to deceive the people of Corinth the way you're doing. If you really can't afford to give to such a worthy cause as ours, and yet you appear so rich to everybody in town—

"I don't think I'm saying what I really mean. But it seems to me that your refusal to help out in this program to build—to develop the youth of Corinth—the President's Physical Fitness Program—well, I'd think it would reflect on your family—on the mayor, on your lovely wife and daughters. If you're too poor—"

Larry was being shifty-eyed during his recital, but his attention was jerked back to Hopkins's face when he heard his adversary develop a hacking cough—the effects of the cigar, no doubt. Only, Bruce Hopkins was not coughing. He was laughing at Larry's performance.

"Look, Shelton," he said, still chuckling. "That crap might have some effect on my wife and daughters, but it leaves me stone cold."

"Not a very good pitch, huh?" Larry dropped all pretense and joined Hopkins in his laughter.

194

"Not bad," Hopkins said, "for suckers, maybe. But it's not worth a damn in this office. Want to try another one?"

"Would it be worth my time? A little polite blackmail, for instance?"

"Like the way you trapped my brother into heading your fund drive? That won't work here, Shelton. There are no witnesses."

"So I notice. But there's still the press outside. I might think up something, with fifty thousand dollars at stake."

"Ten thousand," Hopkins corrected him. "I've already been evaluated. I might think up something better—for both of us." He tightened his eyelids and shifted the cigar to a corner of his mouth. It was coming, whatever it was.

"What's your percentage, Shelton?" As if the mayor had not already told him.

"Fifteen per cent of the gross," Larry said.

"And fifteen per cent of ten thousand is fifteen hundred. Right?"

"Right."

"O.K. You're in business. I'm in business. Related. You raise money for public buildings. I build public buildings. We both take our cut. Right?"

"Right," Larry agreed.

"So why don't we eliminate the middleman? Why don't I write you a check—you personally—for fifteen hundred dollars? You get out of here, call off your dogs, and forget all about me and the reflections on my family." He laughed at that. He relaxed a little, too. "How's my pitch?"

"Interesting," Larry admitted.

"I thought it would be. You're just about as dedicated to the President's Physical Fitness Program as I am. What say?"

Larry took out his cardcase and handed a business card to Bruce Hopkins.

"Make it payable to my company," he said.

"Yeah, that would be better. Shrewd operator."

"Type everything but your signature," Larry cautioned

him. "Or I'll do it, if you can't use that machine. No witnesses."

"No witnesses." Hopkins nodded wisely. He produced a blank check, and Larry typed it as agreed. Hopkins signed. All Larry had to do was cash it—and rot in the state penitentiary, Big Jack and Bruce Hopkins's home-state jailhouse.

Back at Campaign Headquarters Larry immediately endorsed the check over to the Federal Physical Fitness Foundation, Corinth Fund, and put it into an envelope, to which he added another dozen or so Golden Givers' donations during the week.

Shortly before ten on Friday morning he took the envelope over to Sybil Jones at the Golden Givers table.

"I have a little chore for you, Mrs. Jones," he said, "if you have a few minutes to spare."

"Of course, Mr. Shelton." The pink-and-white cherub brightened, eager to be useful. "What is it?"

"This bunch of checks from Golden Givers—your department. As you know, we publish the names of Golden Givers every Sunday, but we don't do it unless they say it's all right.

"I thought you might know some or all of these people. Would you mind calling them and asking permission to publish their names and amounts?"

"Not at all, Mr. Shelton, I'd love to, in fact."

He left her smiling and returned to his executive desk. It was half an hour before Sybil Jones approached him timidly.

"Mr. Shelton," she said, her brows puckered and her china-blue eyes worried.

"Yes?"

"Aren't Golden Gifts supposed to be ten thousand dollars and above?"

"Yes, why?"

"Well, here's one from Bruce Hopkins for only fifteen hundred."

"Let me see it." He looked quite surprised, and as puzzled as Sybil Jones, when he had examined the check.

"Don't you suppose there has been some mistake?" she asked.

"I'm sure of it," Larry said. "I called on Mr. Hopkins myself. I understood that he was giving fifteen *thousand*. I merely left a card with him. His girl must have made a mistake when she mailed in the check. I see it's made out to my firm."

"Shall I call him and ask? I know Bruce and Charlotte. I'm sure they intended to give more than this."

"Would you?" Larry asked eagerly. "You may use my phone."

Sybil Jones sat down in the stenographer's chair and dialed the Hopkins Construction Company. A moment later she got the boss.

"Bruce?" she said. "This is Sybil—Sybil Jones."

She paused, then said, "I'm just calling to clear up a little mistake your secretary must have made.

"I'm at Campaign Headquarters, and I have a check from you for fifteen hundred dollars. It's in the Golden Givers file, and they're supposed to be ten thousand dollars and up. You did mean fifteen *thousand*, didn't you, Bruce?"

Larry would have given a lot to hear the other end of the conversation, but he had to settle for the happy smile which spread over the cherub's features.

"I was sure that was it, Bruce. A slight mistake," Sybil said after a time. "Just an error by your secretary. So you'll have her send us another check? For fifteen thousand. . . .

"Yes—the Federal Physical Fitness Foundation, Corinth Fund . . .

"Yes—I'll destroy this check myself—personally . . .

"Yes, I'm at his desk now, using his telephone. Want me to put him on?" . . .

"Bruce wants to speak to you, Mr. Shelton. He'll explain everything."

She handed him the telephone and stood up, delighted at having proved so useful.

"Shelton speaking." Larry watched Sybil Jones tear up the evidence on her way back to the Golden Givers table.

"God damn you, Shelton," Hopkins raged. "I should have known better than to trust a crook like you."

"I'm sorry I underestimated you, Mr. Hopkins."

"Underestimated me! You—"

"I'll revise the evaluation made by our committee."

Larry hung up on the mayor's brother. He resented the reflections being cast on his family, especially the alleged relations between him and his mother.

26

$ $ $

WEIGHING IN AT SOMETHING OVER EIGHT HUNDRED THOUSAND dollars on the morning of November 18, Mr. Fiz Fit was beginning to look like a healthy youngster. But, except for the gift from clearinghouse association still to be reported by the Bank Busters, he had already received about all the cream he was going to get, and the hard milking was well under way. The All-Stars, the Gold Diggers, and the Homebodies were turning in bags of small change regularly. The Christian Knights had raised fifteen thousand dollars in their one-shot Health Offering.

After the Shawn Brother's report on Saturday, Larry had

presented his New York staff's analysis of the campaign and projections for the last two weeks.

"We are about even," he had said to the council. "The gleanings, if assiduously gathered, should put us over.

"The Solid Citizens are not through yet—a few more hundred-dollar gifts. Charlie should get the finals on the service clubs this week, and Claire Milliken and I will be working the women's clubs.

"After that, it will be up to our Bell Ringers to boost us over the top in their house-to-house canvass next week."

"But we will make it?" Helen Boatwright could always be depended upon to inject a shot of anxiety.

"According to our projections we should be close, barring some unforeseen difficulties or unexpected calamity." Larry deliberately made his smile a wan one.

He was all enthusiasm, however, at the Bell Ringers' Rally held on Monday morning in the city auditorium, the only hall in town large enough to hold that swarm of locusts whose job it was to garner the last few grains from the cut-over stubble.

"You are the true Bell Ringers," he told them. "The ones to alert every man, woman, and child in Corinth to his opportunity to participate in this wonderful project. Ten dollars, five dollars, a dollar, a quarter, a dime, or a nickel—his gift, if only a penny, will give him a kind of immortality, an interest in this great program for the health of the nation.

"Call on every house in your block once, twice, three times—until you know that every single citizen of Corinth, young or old—even the more intelligent pets—is wearing a Fiz Fit button in his lapel—or on his license-tag collar.

"Do that and you may be assured that Corinth will have one of the finest public gymnasiums in the nation.

"Now, go out and show the President that Corinth is behind him one hundred per cent in his National Physical Fitness program."

The meeting was over by ten o'clock. Claire Milliken was waiting for Larry in the wings when he came offstage.

After his usual post-rally business with overeager Bell Ringers, she led him to her car in the municipal parking lot.

"We'll just about make it to the Dianas' luncheon in time for me to introduce you to a few of the girls before we eat," Claire said on the way to the car.

"I hope I didn't keep you waiting too long," Larry apologized. "But there are always some in the audience who want to get our instructions perfectly straight in their minds."

"Oh, it wasn't the Bell Ringers. I thought I'd never get you away from Dora Mansfield." She said it in strained voice, and laughed a little nervously as she unlocked her car. She just did not know how to begin. "Dora's monopolized you for two or three whole weeks. But this is our week, isn't it?"

"It certainly is," Larry said, making a gesture of helping her into the driver's seat. The muscles in her arm were taut.

"I've been looking forward to it," she said, as he closed her door.

"So have I—eagerly." He went around to his side and got in.

"Most of the clubs have their own pet charities," Claire began, once the motor was purring, "but we all have our benevolences budgets, too, for special things. I'm sure you'll raise a sizable amount this week."

"*We'll* raise it, you mean," he said. "This is *our* week, and I'm depending on you to make it a success. I'm just a consultant, you know."

She laughed. Her initial nervousness was subsiding just perceptibly.

The Dianas held their luncheon in a small banquet room at the Corinth Woman's Club. The Penelopes poured tea at one of the country clubs. The Echoes made Larry their Narcissus for the evening back at the Woman's Club.

Larry could hardly tell one group from another. The Mesdames Chairmen looked alike, spoke alike, gushed alike. The Secretaries intoned the minutes with the same carefully cultivated diction. The Parliamentarians pronounced identical judgments on Points of Order, and the Historians' harlequin glasses had all been cast in one mold.

But somebody had misjudged Claire Milliken. That somebody was either J. Samuel Algood or Laurence P. Shelton—possibly John D. Milliken, who according to J. Samuel Algood had established several homes away from home, for reasons which Laurence P. Shelton had doubted from the moment he first saw Claire and which he was distrusting increasingly with every trip from Campaign Headquarters to luncheon to tea to cocktail party to dinner. If Claire Milliken was a frigid matron, the exercise was certainly thawing her out. From timid, half-embarrassed introductions to various Dianas on Monday she progressed to easily informal give-and-take on Tuesday, to jokingly announced hesitancy at sharing her prize catch with envious rivals on Wednesday, to blatant exhibitionism in presenting her man to the Council of Federated Women's Clubs on Thursday evening.

In their numerous rides together Claire's temperature rose steadily until noon Wednesday, when she held onto Larry as possessively as a three-year-old with her first talking doll. Thereafter, although her outward show continued toward its peak, her manner in the car cooled and tightened to the point where Larry felt again the original tenseness in her arm when he opened her car door for her after the council meeting. This girl needed help. She just did not know how to carry on, and she was near desperation.

Larry had his problems too. He had to back his judgment again, soon, or lose his self-confidence. If he had miscalculated Claire Milliken, if he had been wrong in what, how much, and when she would give, he was losing his touch. According to his analyses and projections, the night of the council meeting of Federated Women's Clubs of Corinth should have been the night—the high point of the week, *their* week, his and Claire's. The *when* was upon him. But what, and how much? Well, solicitation was his business.

"Claire," he said, as she was preparing to back out of

her parking space, "with all due respects to the lovely ladies of Corinth, I've had about all the woman food and ladies' drinks that I can stand in one week. Isn't there somewhere we can go for and get an honest-to-god drink of whiskey? Preferably Scotch."

"Let me think." It seemed that something in her relaxed, at least momentarily. "I don't think we should be seen in a bar this late. John's out of town. I could take you to the house for a drink, but—"

She waited to release the brake and engage the transmission. She practically held her breath while she deliberated for a full minute. Then she made her decision.

"Yes," she said. "I think I know a place."

Claire backed her car out and drove to a large complex of studio and bachelors' apartments not far from the Woman's Club. She drove unerringly to a vacant garage space in the rear, Number 28C.

With equal confidence she opened a back door to one of the residence buildings with a key which she took from her purse, and led the way to an automatic elevator. On the third floor she turned left, then right, down a corridor, to Number 28C, for which she also had a key. Indirect lamps revealed a sumptuous studio apartment illuminated in the daytime only by a skylight.

"We should be able to find a drink here," she said, as Larry helped her off with her coat. She was still tense, but trying.

"Make yourself comfortable, Larry," she added. "I'll see what's in the kitchen."

Larry hung up their coats and sat down on a sofa, where he lit a cigarette and settled back to case the hideaway. It was all too patently a man's apartment. Evidently Sam knew only one side of the Milliken household, and that not the distaff. Claire just might have unplumbed depths.

She returned with a tray holding glasses, ice, Scotch, and bottled soda.

202

"Look what I found," she said.

"Exactly what I ordered." He rose from the sofa.

"Sit where you are. I'll pour. Say when."

"When." Larry let her indulge in her generosity before he called his shot.

She mixed his drink and poured one for herself. Then she handed him his glass and sat down beside him.

"If you're wondering," she said a little later, "this is not my place. It's my husband's. I found out about it some time ago, and—well—I had duplicates made of his keys and came to see what it was like."

Larry made no comment. They could see very well what it was like. It was just right.

"Music?" Claire asked after a second drink from the spring.

"Yes. I think I'd like that."

Claire took her glass with her to the console of a stereophonic sound system. Larry followed her and looked over her shoulder while she examined a collection of album jackets.

"Strings?" she asked.

"By all means." He moved closer, to read the titles, and to touch her body—tense, but not shrinking from his.

"How's this?" She turned her face up for confirmation. She was trying. It was just that she had never learned how.

"Fine." He smiled, but made no move. Give her time.

They chose several more records, and she put a stack on the record changer. She knew her way around the place—she had been there more than once, but alone, certainly. When the music started—the volume was already set—they returned to the sofa, pausing long enough en route to refill their glasses.

"Was this what you had in mind at the Woman's Club?" Claire asked when they were settled again.

"Exactly." He left the hideaway, the Scotch, and the music to their appointed tasks.

At that, he was a little premature. Her first kiss was cool —tight-lipped and timorous. But in time he worked his way through the outer inhibitions. After his self-confidence had begun to rise again, he asked, "Shall I mix another drink, or—"

"Not another drink. It won't be necessary." She smiled —bravely it seemed. "I made my decision before we left the Woman's Club."

She offered a hand, for him to help her to her feet.

The music was playing in the bedroom, too, and would be for some time. Claire began to undress as deliberately as she had made her decision in the parking lot at the Woman's Club.

"Want to help?" she asked when she got down to the essentials—he was way ahead of her. He helped. Claire Milliken had merely read of such things; but, by God, she was trying. Spunky.

She was still trying when he turned her bare body to his. She had to quit trying. It might take all the gentleness, all the tenderness, he could muster; but she had to stop trying. And finally she did stop, after he had petted her and fondled her half an hour. When she did give, she was not trying at all. She was not even aware that she was giving. But he found out what it was she had to give—something John D. Milliken had never found, or John D. Milliken was a damn fool.

"Was I absolutely horrid, Larry?" She asked as she lay completely relaxed in his arms.

"You were wonderful."

"Thank you, Larry. Would you like to know why I'm asking?"

"If you want to tell me, yes."

"I do want to tell you. I think I should. You may not like it."

"As you wish." Larry liked it already.

"I told you this was John's place. I can't really blame him. It's all my fault."

"Impossible," Larry said.

"No it isn't. I've been a frigid wife. I know it. But I couldn't help it.

204

"My mother died when I was born. I've always known about it. I grew up with it. My father kept me reminded of it. And when I married, I—I didn't want to die, like my mother."

She shuddered slightly. Larry involuntarily tightened his arms, hugged her to him. He could love this woman.

"I tried. God knows I tried."

"I know, too," Larry said. "You tried with me—at first. You must never try again."

"But I did. I really tried, every time John—but I always froze up. It couldn't have been any pleasure to him. So I don't blame him. Do you mind my telling you this, Larry?"

"Not at all. I'm flattered—grateful."

"But I'm not through. This is what will hurt. It isn't you, Larry—yes, it is, to some extent—but it might have been anyone. I had to try again."

"You did. But stop trying," Larry warned her again.

"That's not what I mean. I've been taking those new pills. You know—you've read about them. I've been taking them for two years. My doctor has made every test he knows of, and he is positive that I couldn't—that with them I'm in no danger. They have worked perfectly with his other patients—those who are—practicing. Do you understand me, Larry?"

"Yes. I think so."

"I've had every test but this one. I thought I had complete confidence in the pills, but I had to find out before—before I went back to John.

"I love John, and I can't risk losing him again if I ever—two years is a long time."

She turned so that her eyes were looking in Larry's.

"You see why I had to tell you, Larry? I'm being honest. I had to try someone, and—well—I really do like you a lot—but you'll be gone in another two weeks. There couldn't be anything permanent between us.

"So I had to explain. I'm not ashamed, not about this. I'm ashamed of what I've done to you. I've *used* you, Larry, and I'm sorry—if I've hurt you."

Fair enough, Larry thought. Use and be used. But he was not entirely happy about it. He could have loved this woman.

"Don't feel too bad," she went on. "You've been so considerate, so gentle, so tender. I only hope John—Anyway I'm grateful, deeply grateful. I owe you a lot. I'll do everything I can to repay you."

She made the overtures that time, without half trying. Her confidence in those new pills seemed complete.

In a talkative mood again, she asked, "Am I as good as Dora Mansfield?"

"How would I know?"

"Gallant!" She could be playful. "I know that you know. I know that John knows, too. I think she was his first one. I would get a world of satisfaction out of thinking that I had taken you away from her.

"I'd like for her to know it, too. And John—I think I'd like for him to know. I can see to it that Dora finds out. But John—I don't know. I guess I'm kind of crazy."

She turned in his arms again.

"Promise me you won't go back to Dora," she pleaded. "I know I have no right to tell you where to go or where not to go. I shouldn't care where—but I'm afraid I do care. Dora can't mean much to you, and you'll be gone in two weeks. Promise me you won't return to her."

"I think I can give you every assurance in the world that I will never go back to Dora Mansfield."

Her gratitude was surpassed only by her confidence in those new pills.

206

27

$ $ $

LARRY FELT LIKE WHISTLING WHILE HE WORKED AT CAMPAIGN Headquarters Friday morning. He was every inch the old master again. All the various committees had been briefed. His entire schedule was on time. The rest of the fund drive was coasting in—stripping the last few drops into the milk pail. He had one more woman's club to address, another evening meeting. Claire would be on hand for the introduction—and later. John D. Milliken would be out of town until Thanksgiving, and Larry had hopes, and reasons to believe, that Claire's gratitude would hold out until his return. Anyway, she needed all the expert briefing she could get before she tried to re-seduce her own husband.

Of course, there was still Pat. Larry had intended to give more time to her during this campaign. But as soon as it was over he would call her in to New York—Scotty and Red, and Sam, too, if they wanted to come. He had recruited a good team. With a little time in a new office, a little polishing up here and there, they would be ready for their next assignment. And on his home ground, he could get Pat into proper perspective, find out what made her tick. Once she became aware, she could be just what he wanted. She was only a kid. By the time she reached the age of Dora Mansfield and Claire Milliken—

"Are you sure there isn't someone we can picket?" Helen Boatwright was doing a solo-picket job at his desk.

"I don't think so, Helen. Don't you feel that we'll make it without getting angry at anyone?"

"But, Larry." First-naming came hard for Helen. "I feel I've done so little."

"You've done a fine job. Look at the success we're having. You're a part of it, a big part of every bit of it."

"I suppose so, but I feel so left out. We've had no demonstrations—I'm good at that."

"You're just feeling let down, now that the big excitement is dying out." He looked at his watch. "It's after twelve, Helen. Why don't we have lunch together?"

"Oh." She was easily astounded. "Why, yes, Mr.—Larry —I'd love to."

Larry cleared off his desk and took Helen down to the coffee shop. She was niggardly in her order, but ate ravenously when the food came.

"You're positive now that we have it made, aren't you, Larry?" she asked over coffee.

"No, not positive. We're within a hundred thousand of our goal, I'm sure. But we have to go well over a million to pay all expenses and still net that amount. We won't know before the end of next week." He might as well leave her some anxiety. She enjoyed it so.

"Is there anything that could block us now?" She was looking for trouble.

"Not that I can think of."

But there was. A minute later the house music went off, and a voice came over the sound system.

"We have a news bulletin of unprecedented importance. The President of the United States has just been shot—assassinated. Repeat: The President of the United States has

208

just been shot. That's all we know. We will keep you informed as we receive subsequent bulletins."

"Oh, my God," Helen said. "It can't be true. Why would anyone—" Then she burst into tears, as did other women at tables all around them.

Larry himself was too completely stunned by the announcement to pay much attention to his companion. He had known violence. In Korea he had seen men killed, had perhaps killed men himself—he never knew. But assassination, even in petty gangland feuds, was more than he could stomach. And needless, useless, heartless political assassination—

Was it political? It had to be. The President. It was some time before the full personal impact hit Larry, the effect on the campaign, on him. Well, he was ready to throw in the towel. The campaign was now a trivial thing. Forget it.

When he recovered enough to dismiss the fund drive, he saw that Helen was bordering on hysteria. What could he do?

He reached across the table and patted her arm awkwardly.

"It's tough, hard to take, Helen. Maybe it was a mistake, just a rumor."

"No. No, I know it's true. He was too good to live, too wonderful—"

"There was no mention of his being killed—just shot."

"He's dead. He'll die. And just when I—we—were doing this work for him, too. It isn't fair. If he had only lived to see our job finished."

Larry patted her again and watched her closely for signs of recovery. Let her keep talking; that was the way.

"He would have loved the gymnasium. We might even have got him to come here to dedicate it." Her voice was low, musing. She was voicing her dreams. At a time like this her sobs were as much for the gymnasium as for the President. In her it was sincerity. Coming from himself it would have been—To hell with it.

"Can you walk now?" Larry asked. You walked a drunk;

you walked a sleeping-pill case. That was what she sounded like. "We should be getting back upstairs."

"Yes. Oh, yes, I can walk."

Larry helped her to her feet.

"I suppose we should call an emergency meeting of the council," he said on the way up to the mezzanine. "This of course changes the complexion of our entire campaign, certainly its timing. We might as well call it off, or try again at some more propitious moment."

"We can't quit," Helen said with somewhat more spirit. "He wouldn't want us to."

By that time they had reached the ballroom.

They found Campaign Headquarters in complete silence, except for the voice on the sound system reading the second bulletin. The President had indeed been shot. His condition was not known. His car was rushing him to a hospital.

At the end of the announcement Larry spoke to the campaign workers.

"This is all for today. I'm sure most of you want to go home. You may go—all except the telephone committee." It was no time to refer to them as Call Girls. "We'll ask the ones here to stay on and the other shifts to keep coming on at their regular times.

"They are our communications network. Frankly, I won't know where we stand or what we'll do next until the council meets. So please stay on the job to keep the rest of us informed.

"This is the greatest tragedy that could have befallen our country. I don't know when we will meet again—tomorrow, Monday, Tuesday, or never. We'll just have to wait and see. We'll keep you informed."

Larry turned without any further word of dismissal and walked to his desk. Pat was at the gymnasium. No one was hovering except Helen Boatwright, and she would be of no immediate help.

Nell Hargreaves came to his desk.

"I'm not leaving," she said. "Neither is Hilda. Is there anything we can do?"

"Ask Hilda to look after Helen," he said. "She's taking it pretty hard. And try to get in touch with Stanley Hogan. He'll probably want to call the council into session. Get Sam Algood, too."

Campaign Headquarters emptied rapidly, except for the permanent secretaries and the Call Girls on duty. The telephones seldom rang. Everyone listened to the house music, with its frequent breaks for additional bulletins. There was little conversation. Only Nell Hargreaves's quiet, efficient voice could be heard calling first Stanley Hogan and then the other council members.

By the time the council met at five, the truth was known. The President was dead.

"I have never opened a sadder meeting," Stanley Hogan began. "And I hope I never have to. What do we do, Larry?"

"I don't know. This is the calamity no one of us could have foreseen. I'm as much at a loss as the rest of you."

"Shall we go on with the campaign, or—" Stan floundered.

"Of course we shall," Helen Boatwright said, softly but positively. "It is what he would have wanted. We *must* go on, and"—she hesitated—"if a motion is in order, I move that we dedicate the gymnasium to his memory, name it after him, a monument to—" She choked up.

So that had been Helen's dream. It was still her dream. Nothing could stand in the way of it. Not even—

"I second the motion." Dr. Rankin's voice never sounded more sonorous.

"What a wonderful thought, Helen," Claire Milliken said, her own eyes moist.

Larry looked around him in amazement. If an old pro had made the same suggestion he would have been blackballed forever by the NAFR, as cynically commercial as that brotherhood might be. But these innocents, these sincere solid citizens,

211

were inaugurating a drive which would make his s.o.b. campaign smell of roses.

"I have a second," Stan said. "Does anyone wish to speak to the motion?"

"Question." In concert.

"All in favor say, 'Aye.'"

It was unanimous.

Still in something of a daze, Larry watched Sam rise and ease out of the conference room.

"My firm is putting a memorial box in Sunday's paper," Charlie Shanks volunteered. "I think perhaps this body should do the same."

"Do you so move?" Stan asked.

"I so move."

"I second," Helen said, her voice still small.

The vote was unanimously affirmative again.

"We'll let Sam Algood word it," Stan suggested.

The telephone rang.

"Take it, Dora," Larry said. "You're nearest to it."

Dora listened for a minute or two and then said, "Thank you, Sybil. I'll tell him."

"It was for you, Larry," Dora said, putting the receiver down. "It was Sybil Jones. She had just heard a news flash announcing that we had decided to dedicate the gymnasium to the late President. She and Aaron are doubling their gift."

"News flash?" Charlie Shanks was astounded. "Oh, sure. Sam Algood. He's really on the ball. I hadn't even missed him."

"I saw him go," Dora said, looking at Larry as though she credited him with sending Sam on his mission.

He was sure then that he could make good his promise never to return to her bed. He was beginning to see the effect this amateur-run fund drive was likely to have on him personally.

"I'll double my gift, too," Helen Boatwright said.

212

That makes it ten dollars, Larry thought. He could feel no enthusiasm.

"Me, too," Stan joined in.

Fifty bucks in all. At least this new breed of money hunters were gulling themselves along with the rest of Corinth's citizenry.

Miss Fanny and Dora Mansfield did not indulge in any such loose talk, and none of the others spoke up immediately.

"Good work, Sam," Charlie Shanks said, as Sam Algood re-entered the room. "It's already on the air. We had a call from Mrs. Jones—Mrs. Aaron Jones. She heard it and phoned Larry."

Sam said nothing, but he looked sheepish. He knew what the innocents were up to, even if they did not.

"We want you to word a memorial to go into the Sunday papers, Sam," Stan said. "We decided on it while you were out. I'll talk to you about it."

Sam nodded.

"Well, I guess that's about all." Stan faced the body. "Do I hear a move to adjourn?"

He heard one.

Claire came up to Larry on her way out.

"Our club dinner has been canceled," she said.

It was not *their* dinner. It was a Delphians' dinner; but Larry knew what she meant.

The memorial box appeared in both Sunday papers as a full page, edged in black, presenting a brief proclamation to the effect that the Physical Fitness Council of Corinth had, on this date, resolved to dedicate the new gymnasium to the memory of their beloved President and to name it in his honor. A discreet sentence in parentheses at the bottom of the page expressed sincere thanks to those donors who had already seen fit to double their original gifts.

The remaining week of the fund drive ran its course almost without direction. The Call Girls kept the telephones humming. The various tables, from the Solid Citizens down, were swamped with mail and drop-in givers. The Bell Ringers carried out the most phenomenally successful house-to-house canvass ever conducted in the city.

Other than feeding spot announcements to radio and TV stations all week long, there was little for Larry to do personally. Wednesday he received a letter from Katy, or rather an envelope containing nothing but the full-page memorial torn from Sunday's *Corinthian*. Below the council's resolution Katy had printed large, in red pencil, the one word: *GHOUL*. He smiled grimly at her accusation. For once he was innocent. The worst that could be truthfully said of him was that he had been a fellow traveler. But that was not the worst that would be said, enviously perhaps, around the NAFR campfires. His legend was growing.

He attended Thanksgiving dinner at the old laundry— a feast again supplied by the Corinth Press Club and prepared by Momma and Angelo.

Friday, John D. and Claire Milliken came by his desk to up their gift to twenty thousand dollars. Both looked happy— over the years John D. would probably save the extra ten thousand from the rent he might otherwise have been paying on Apartment 28C. Larry felt a pang of jealousy as the affectionate couple departed. John D. Milliken did not deserve her.

Campaign Headquarters closed at noon Saturday, but it was four o'clock before Shawn Brothers, both of them, were ready with a trial audit of the fund drive. According to their current figures, the gross came to $1,533,062.69.

"Of course, there are some funds still to be accounted for," one of the brothers continued. "We have word from Mr. Phillips that several thousand dollars have been sent directly to the Foundation in New Jersey, and not all committees here in Corinth have made their final reports."

Larry spent all of Sunday morning trying to analyze the report sheets:

214

Golden Givers	$640,000.00
Big Boys	212,000.00
Company Men	172,000.00
Bank Busters	156,000.00
Solid Citizens	64,800.00
Gold Diggers	15,412.13
All Stars	14,331.46
Christian Knights	15,510.10
Bell Ringers	163,162.50
Roll Callers	10,112.34
White Collar Girls	15,104.91
Homebodies	1,416.25
Mail Men	11,202.00
Service Clubs	9,416.00
Women's Clubs	6,687.00
Drop-Ins	10,408.00
Anonymous	15,500.00
Total	$1,533,062.69

The Bell Ringers' take was certainly far out of line, and he would have to see details of the gift-doubling before he could make a comparative study; but he felt reasonably sure that he would have gone well over his million even without the calamity which had befallen the nation.

He was fairly certain, too, that the final figures would top $1,600,000. And fifteen per cent of that was $240,000. He was still in business. His *modus operandi* was sound. He could put seventy-five or eighty thousand back into the foundation— an adequate nut for continued operations.

Pat, Sam, and Scotty came to Suite 312, by appointment, shortly after two o'clock.

"O.K., kids," Larry said, after he had seated them. "It's all over but the shouting, and we can leave that to the Physical Fitness Council of Corinth."

215

"I've already been shouting," Pat said exuberantly, "and I feel like shouting forever. It was such a surprise—going so far beyond the goal."

"What did you expect?" Larry asked.

"I guess I expected it. I knew you were wonderful, Larry. But I guess I was afraid to hope for too much. I'm like that."

"Now we can have everything," Scotty said. "The world is ours."

"I think you're right, Scotty," Larry agreed. "That's why I called you in. It's time to talk about the future."

"A glorious future," Pat said, still beaming.

"Yes. It looks that way. We can start closing out here. We'll let the laundry go before Christmas. You kids can take a vacation and come to New York after the holidays. We'll start work on the next project. I already have a spot picked out."

His plans met with complete silence. Pat exchanged glances with Scotty. Sam watched Larry, and grinned.

"Oh, no, Larry." Pat broke the silence. "We can't leave here. We're just beginning."

"According to my schedule we have just finished," Larry said firmly. "Of course, there's a bonus for all three of you—Red, too—and I think with your year of experience you might be worth twice your present salaries. Herb will agree."

"It isn't money, Larry. We haven't been working for money."

"I have," Larry said. Damn it. How was he ever going to get through to this girl? She was worth her weight—perfect for her height and age—in gold to Laurence P. Shelton Associates.

"There you go again," she said indulgently, but her brow puckered into a frown as she continued. "We know how wonderful you've been to us. We appreciate all you've done for us, but we can't leave Corinth. We just can't.

"We've talked it over." She glanced at Sam and Scotty again. "We've discussed it with the council. They've agreed to take over the laundry and operate it until the new gym is completed. They want us to stay on—to operate the new one —to staff it. We have to do that, Larry. It's our life."

Pat lowered her eyes and reached out to Scotty for support.

He grasped her hand in his.

"Pat's right, Mr. Shelton," he said. "We're taking a vacation during the holidays, all right. We're going on our honeymoon."

"Yes, Larry," Pat said, looking up again. "We're being married Christmas. But we'll be back on the job here by mid-January."

Larry shrugged his shoulders and slumped back into his desk chair.

"Well. I guess that's that," he said. "You may consider these checks as wedding presents instead of bonuses."

He reached into his desk drawer and took out two checks for a thousand dollars each—made out to the happy pair.

Pat and Scotty rose to accept the checks, and they did not sit down again.

"I told Scotty you would take it all right," Pat said, somewhat ruefully. "I'm sorry, Larry. This is the way it had to be."

"Sure. I understand."

"Really?" She brightened again.

"Really."

They said goodbye and left Suite 312.

Larry turned to Sam Algood.

"I have a bonus check for you, too, Sam. And a thousand dollars in currency, to pay my laundry bill."

He fished another check and a sealed envelope out of his drawer and handed them to Sam.

"Pick up that shirt, and be sure the cuff is clean," Larry said.

"Sure thing."

"Now, how about you, Sam? Do you feel like moving

along with me to greener pastures? You've done yeoman service here."

"No, BTO." Sam remained standing too. "I wouldn't be worth much in a strange town. I wouldn't know my way around."

"What will you do here?"

"I have an idea that Pat and Scotty can find a place for me when they start staffing their new gym. For me and Red both—a little jetsam for us flotsam to hang onto. We need those kids."

"Is that enough?" Larry asked.

"I have another string to my bow. You know what every newshound's ambition is, don't you?"

"No, what is it?"

"To write a novel. Thanks to you, I've had the leisure and subsidy to do that this last year. An agent friend of mine likes what I've sent him. I've just been waiting around to write the final chapters."

"A novel?" Larry said. "What's it about?"

"I think we'll call it *The Money Hunters*." Sam grinned, his biggest grin ever.

"Well, I'll be damned." Larry chuckled.

"Undoubtedly," Sam said, his hand already on the doorknob. "But when you go to hell, BTO, I'm sure you'll have no trouble at all raising funds to air-condition the place."

THE END